LIZARD

LIZARD

Banana Yoshimoto

Translated from the Japanese by Ann Sherif

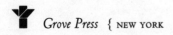

Grove Press { NEW YORK

FIRST EDITION

Library of Congress Cataloging-in-Publication Data

Yoshimoto, Banana, 1964–
    [Tokage. English]
    Lizard / by Banana Yoshimoto; translated from the Japanese by
Ann Sherif.—1st ed.
   ISBN 0-8021-1564-0
   I. Sherif, Ann.
  PL865.07138T6513   1995   895.6'35—dc20   94-32007

Design by Laura Hammond Hough

Grove Press
841 Broadway
New York, NY 10003

10 9 8 7 6 5 4 3 2 1

CONTENTS

NEWLYWED

Once, just once, I met the most incredible person on the train. That was a while ago, but I still remember it vividly.

At the time, I was twenty-eight years old, and had been married to Atsuko for about one month.

I had spent the evening downing whiskey at a bar with my buddies and was totally smashed by the time I got on the train to head home. For some reason, when I heard them announce my stop, I stayed put, frozen in my seat.

It was very late, and I looked around and saw that there were only three other passengers in the car. I wasn't so far gone that I didn't realize what I'd done. I had stayed on the train because I didn't really feel like going home.

In my drunken haze, I watched as the familiar platform of my station drew near. The train slowed down, and came to a stop. As the doors slid open, I could feel a blast of cool night air rush into the car, and then the doors again closed so firmly that I thought they had been sealed for all eternity. The train started to move, and I could see the neon signs of my neighborhood stores flash by outside the train window. I sat quietly and watched them fade into the distance.

A few stations later, the man got on. He looked like an old homeless guy, with ragged clothes, long, matted hair, and a beard—plus he smelled really strange. As if on cue, the other three passengers stood up and moved to neighboring cars, but I missed my chance to escape, and instead stayed where I was, seated right in the middle of the car. I didn't have a problem with the guy anyway, and even felt a trace of contempt for the other passengers, who had been so obvious about avoiding him.

Oddly enough, the old man came and sat right next to me. I held my breath and resisted the urge to look in his direction. I could see our reflections in the window facing us: the image of two men sitting side by side superimposed over the dazzling city lights and the dark of the night. I almost felt like laughing when I saw how anxious I looked there in the window.

"I suppose there's some good reason why you don't want to go home," the man announced in a loud, scratchy voice.

At first, I didn't realize that he was talking to me, maybe because I was feeling so oppressed by the stench emanating from his body. I closed my eyes and pretended to be asleep, and then I heard him whisper, directly into my left ear, "Would you like to tell me why you're feeling so reluctant about going home?"

There was no longer any mystery about whom he was addressing, so I screwed my eyes shut even more firmly. The rhythmical sound of the train's wheels clicking along the tracks filled my ears.

"I wonder if you'll change your mind when you see me like this," he said.

Or I thought that's what he said, but the voice changed radically, and zipped up into a much higher pitch, as if someone had fast-forwarded a tape. This sent my head reeling, and everything around me seemed to rush into a different space, as the stench of the man's body disappeared, only to be replaced by the light, floral scent of perfume. My eyes still closed, I recognized a range of new smells: the warm fragrance of a woman's skin, mingled with fresh summer blossoms.

I couldn't resist; I had to take a look. Slowly, slowly, I opened my eyes, and what I saw almost gave me a heart attack. Inexplicably, there was a woman seated where the homeless guy had been, and the man was nowhere to be seen.

Frantic, I looked around to see if anyone else had witnessed this amazing transformation, but the passengers in the neighboring cars seemed miles away, in a totally different space, separated by a transparent wall, all looking just as tired as they had moments before, indifferent to my surprise. I glanced over at the woman again, and wondered what exactly had happened. She sat primly beside me, staring straight ahead.

I couldn't even tell what country she was from. She had long brown hair, gray eyes, gorgeous legs, and wore a black dress and black patent leather heels. I definitely knew that face from somewhere—like maybe she was my favorite actress, or my first girlfriend, or a cousin, or my mother, or an older woman I'd lusted after—her face looked very familiar. And she wore a corsage of fresh flowers, right over her ample breasts.

I bet she's on her way home from a party, I thought, but then it occurred to me again that the old guy had disappeared. Where had he gone, anyway?

"You still don't feel like going home, do you?" she said, so sweetly that I could almost smell it. I tried convincing myself that this was nothing more than a drunken nightmare. That's what it was, an ugly duckling dream, a transformation from bum to beauty. I didn't understand what was happening, but I knew what I saw.

"I certainly don't, with you by my side."

I was surprised at my own boldness. I had let her know exactly what I had on my mind. Even though the train had pulled in to another station and people were straggling on to the neighboring cars, not one single person boarded ours. No one so much as glanced our way, probably because they were too tired and preoccupied. I wondered if they wanted to keep riding and riding, as I did.

"You're a strange one," the woman said to me.

"Don't jump to conclusions," I replied.

"Why not?"

She looked me straight in the eye. The flowers on her breast trembled. She had incredibly thick eyelashes, and big, round eyes, deep and distant, which reminded me of the ceiling of the first planetarium I ever saw as a child: an entire universe enclosed in a small space.

{ { {

"A minute ago, you were a filthy old bum."

"But even when I look like this, I'm pretty scary, aren't I?" she said. "Tell me about your wife."

"She's petite."

I felt as if I were watching myself from far away. What are you doing, talking to a stranger on a train? What is this, true confessions?

"She's short, and slender, and has long hair. And her eyes are real narrow, so she looks like she's smiling, even when she's angry."

Then I'm sure she asked me, "What does she do when you get home at night?"

"She comes down to meet me with a nice smile, as if she were on a divine mission. She'll have a vase of flowers on the table, or some sweets, and the television is usually on. I can tell that she's been knitting. She never forgets to put a fresh bowl of rice on the family altar every day. When I wake up on Sunday mornings, she'll be doing laundry, or vacuuming, or chatting with the lady next door. Every day, she puts out food for the neighborhood cats, and she cries when she watches mushy TV shows.

"Let's see, what else can I tell you about Atsuko? She sings in the bath, and she talks to her stuffed animals when she's dusting them. On the phone with her friends, she laughs hard at anything they say, and, if it's one of her old pals from high school, they'll go on for hours. Thanks to Atsuko's ways, we have a happy home. In fact, sometimes it's so much fun at home that it makes me want to puke."

After this grand speech of mine, she turned and nodded compassionately.

"I can picture it," she said.

I replied, "How could you? What do you know about these things?" to which she smiled broadly. Her smile was nothing like Atsuko's, but still it seemed awfully familiar to me. At that moment, a childhood mem-

Banana Yoshimoto { LIZARD

ory flitted through my head: I'm walking to school with a friend, and we're still just little kids, so we're wearing the kind of school uniforms with shorts, instead of long pants. It's the dead of winter, and our legs are absolutely freezing, and we look at each other, about to complain about the cold, but then we just start laughing instead, because we both know that griping isn't going to make us any warmer. Scenes like that—smiles of mutual understanding—kept flashing through my mind, and I actually started having a good time, on my little train bench.

Then I heard her saying, "How long have you been down here in Tokyo?"

Her question struck me as terribly odd. Why had she said it like that, "down here in Tokyo"?

I asked her, "Hey, are you speaking Japanese? What language are you using?"

She nodded again, and replied, "It's not any language from any one country. They're just words that only you and I can understand. You know, like words you only use with certain people, like with your wife, or an old girlfriend, or your dad, or a friend. You know what I mean, a special type of language that only you and they can comprehend."

"But what if more than two people are talking to one another?"

"Then there'll be a language that just the three of you can understand, and the words will change again if another person joins the conversation. I've been watching this city long enough to know that it's full of people like you, who left their hometowns and came here by themselves. When I meet people who are transplants from other places, I know that I have to use the language of people who never feel quite at home in this big city. Did you know that people who've lived all their lives in Tokyo can't understand that special language? If I run into a older woman who lives alone, and seems reserved, I speak to her in the language of solitude. For men who are out whoring, I use the language of lust. Does that make sense to you?"

"I guess so, but what if the old lady, the horny guy, you, and I all tried to have a conversation?"

"You don't miss anything, do you? If that were to happen, then the four of us would find the threads that tie us together, a common register just for us."

"I get the idea."

"To get back to my original question, how long have you been in Tokyo?"

"I came here when I was eighteen, right after my mother died, and I've been here ever since."

"And your life with Atsuko, how's it been?"

"Well, actually, sometimes I feel like we live in totally different worlds, especially when she goes on and on about the minutiae of our daily lives, anything and everything, and a lot of it's meaningless to me. I mean, what's the big deal? Sometimes I feel like I'm living with the quintessential housewife. I mean, all she talks about is our home."

A cluster of sharply delineated images floated into my mind: the sound of my mother's slippers pattering by my bed when I was very young, the trembling shoulders of my little cousin, who sat sobbing after her favorite cat died. I felt connected to them, despite their otherness, and found solace in the thought of their physical proximity.

"That's how it feels?"

"And how about you? Where are you headed?" I asked.

"Oh, I just ride around and observe. To me, trains are like a straight line with no end, so I just go on and on, you know. I'm sure that most people think of trains as safe little boxes that transport them back and forth between their homes and offices. They've got their commuter passes, and they get on and get off each day, but not me. That's how you think of trains, right?"

"As a safe box that takes me where I need to go, and then home?" I said. "Sure I do, or I'd be too scared to get on the train in the morning—I'd never know where I'd end up."

She nodded, and said, "Of course, and I'm not saying that you should feel the way I do. If you—or anyone on this train, for that matter—thought of life as a kind of train, instead of worrying only about your usual destinations, you'd be surprised how far you could go, just with the money you have in your wallet right now."

"I'm sure you're right."

"That's the kind of thing I have on my mind when I'm on the train."

"I wish I had that kind of time on my hands."

"As long as you're on this train, you're sharing the same space with lots of different people. Some people spend the time reading, others look at the ads, and still others listen to music. I myself contemplate the potential of the train itself."

"But I still don't understand what this transformation's all about."

"I decided to do it because you didn't get off at your usual station and I wanted to find out why. What better way to catch your eye?"

My head was swimming. Who was this being, anyway? What were we talking about? Our train kept stopping and starting, slipping through the black of the night. And there I was, surrounded by the darkness, being carried farther and farther from my home.

This being sitting next to me felt somehow familiar, like the scent of a place, before I was born, where all the primal emotions, love and hate, blended in the air. I also could sense that I would be in danger if I got too close. Deep inside, I felt timid, even scared, not about my own drunkenness or fear that my mind was playing tricks on me, but the more basic sensation of encountering something much larger than myself, and feeling immeasurably small and insignificant by comparison. Like a wild animal would when confronted by a larger beast, I felt the urge to flee for my life.

{ { {

In my stupor, I could hear her saying, "You never have to go back to that station again, if you don't want to. That's one option."

I guess she's right, I thought, but continued to sit there in silence. Rocked by the motion of the train and soothed by the rhythm of the wheels below, I closed my eyes and pondered the situation. I tried to imagine the station near my house and how it looked when I came home in the late afternoon. I recalled the masses of red and yellow flowers whose names I didn't know out in the plaza in front of the station. The bookstore across the way was always packed with people flipping through paperbacks and magazines. All I could ever see was their backs—at least, when I walked past from the direction of the station.

The delicious smell of soup wafted from the Chinese restaurant, and people lined up in front of the bakery, waiting to buy the special cakes they make there. A group of high school girls in their uniforms talk loudly and giggle as they walk ever so slowly across the plaza. It's weird that they're moving at such a leisurely pace. A burst of laughter rises from the group, and some teen-age boys tense up as they walk past. One of the boys, though, doesn't even seem to notice the girls, and walks on calmly. He's a nice-looking guy, and I'd guess that he's popular with the girls. A perfectly made-up secretary passes by, yawning as she walks. She isn't carrying anything, so I imagine that she's on the way back to the office from an errand. I can tell that she doesn't want to go back to work; the weather's too nice for that. A businessman gulping down some vitamin beverage by the kiosk, other people waiting for friends. Some of them are reading paperbacks, others are people watching as they wait.

One finally catches sight of the friend she's been waiting for and runs to greet him. The elderly lady who walks slowly into my field of vision; the line of yellow and green and white taxis at the taxi stand that roar away from the station, one after another. The solid, weathered buildings nearby and the areas flanking the broad avenue.

And when I began to wonder what would happen if I never went back to that station, the whole image in my mind took on the quality of a haunting scene from an old movie, one fraught with meaning. All the living beings there suddenly became objects of my affection. Someday when I die, and only my soul exists, and my spirit comes home on a summer evening during the Bon Buddhist festival, that's probably what the world will look like to me.

And then Atsuko appears, walking slowly toward the station in the summer heat. She has her hair pulled back in a tight bun, even though I've told her that it makes her look dowdy. Her eyelids are so heavy that I wonder whether she can actually see anything, plus she's squinting now because of the glaring sun and her eyes have narrowed down to practically nothing. She's carrying a big bag instead of a shopping basket. She looks hungrily at the stuffed waffles in the little stall by the station, and even pauses for a moment as if she were going to stop and buy one, but then she changes her mind and walks into the drugstore instead. She stands for a long while in front of the shampoo section.

Come on, Atsuko, they're all the same. Just pick one. You look so serious! Shampoo is not something worth wasting time on. But she can't decide and keeps standing there, until a man rushing through the store bumps into her. Atsuko stumbles and then says she's sorry to the man. He bumped into you! You're not the one who should apologize. You should be as hard on him as you are on me.

Finally, Atsuko finds the perfect shampoo, and she takes it up to the cash register, where she starts chatting with the cashier. She's smiling sweetly. She leaves the store, a slender figure of a woman, becoming a mere black line as she recedes into the distance. A tiny black line. But I can tell that she's walking lightly, though slowly, and drinking in the air of this small town.

Our house is Atsuko's universe, and she fills it with small objects, all of her own choosing. She picks each of them as carefully as she did that bottle of shampoo. And then Atsuko comes to be someone who is neither a mother nor a wife, but an entirely different being.

For me, the beautiful, all-encompassing web spun by this creature is at once so polluted, yet so pure that I feel compelled to grab on to it. I am terrified by it but find myself unable to hide from it. At some point I have been caught up in the magical power she has.

"That's the way it is when you first get married." Her words brought me back to my senses. "It's scary to

think of the day when you'll move beyond the honey-
moon stage."

"Yeah, but there's no point dwelling on it now.
I'm still young. Thinking about it just makes me nervous. I'm going home. I'll get off at the next station. At
least I've sobered up a bit."

"I had a good time," she said.

"Me too," I replied, nodding.

The train sped forward, unstoppable, like the
grains of sand in an hourglass timing some precious
event. A voice came booming out of the loudspeaker,
announcing the next stop. We both sat there, not saying
a word. It was hard for me to leave her. I felt as if we'd
been together a very long time.

It seemed as if we had toured Tokyo from every
possible angle, visiting each building, observing every
person, and every situation. It was the incredible sensation of encountering a life force that enveloped everything, including the station near my house, the slight
feeling of alienation I feel toward my marriage and
work and life in general, and Atsuko's lovely profile.
This town breathes in all the universes that people in
this city have in their heads.

Intending to say a few more words, I turned in her direction, only to find the dirty bum sleeping peacefully by my side. Our conversation had come to an end. The train sailed into the station, slowly, quietly, like a ship. I heard the door slide open, and I stood up.

Incredible man, farewell.

TRANSLATOR'S NOTE: "Newlywed" was first serialized on posters aboard Tokyo's Higashi Nippon Japan Railway commuter trains.

LIZARD

I shall refer to her as Lizard here, but not because of the small lizard tattoo that I discovered on her inner thigh.

The woman has round, black eyes that gaze at you with utter detachment, like the eyes of a reptile. Every bend and curve of her small body is cool to the touch, so cool that I want to scoop her up in my two hands.

This may bring to mind the image of a man holding a bunny or a chick, but that's not what I mean. What I imagine is the strange, tickling sensation of sharp claws scampering around in my palms. And then, when I open up my hands to take a peek, a thin, red tongue lashes out. Reflected in those glassy eyes, I see my own lonely face, peering down, looking for something to love and cherish. That's what Lizard feels like to me.

I had already gone to bed and was half asleep when she arrived at my place that night.

"I'm exhausted," she said as she walked in. In the darkness, I could only catch a glimpse of her white coat, but I didn't need to see her face to know that she was in a bad mood. I sat up to look at the clock—it was two in the morning—and was reaching over to turn on the light when I felt her body on top of mine. She buried her face in my chest and slipped her cold hands under my pajama top. I loved the icy feeling of her hands on my bare skin.

I am twenty-nine years old and work as a counselor and therapist in a small hospital for emotionally disturbed children. I've known Lizard for three years. I can't remember when it was, but at some point during our relationship, she stopped talking to nearly everyone but me. I've become her sole outlet, the only person she can relate to.

That night, as always, she lay there on top of me, pressing her face into my chest, right below the collarbone. I felt overwhelmed by the strength of this small woman, who came at me with the force of someone trying to push her way into my body. When she'd collapsed on me like that, I thought for sure that she must be crying, but I was wrong. If anything, she always looked relaxed and refreshed when she finally pulled herself away, her eyes sweet and gentle.

I'm not exactly sure why she liked to do that. Either she used it as a way of getting rid of some unpleasantness from the day—like when you're upset and you flop down on your bed and bury your face in a pillow—or perhaps she was just so exhausted that she didn't want to think anymore, and this was a means of turning her thoughts off.

That particular night, in that dark room, she told me her reasons. "I just wanted you to know that I lost my sight for a while when I was a kid."

"You went blind?" I asked, surprised at this revelation.

"Weird, huh?"

"Yeah. What happened?"

"The doctor said it was psychosomatic. It started when I was five and lasted for three years."

"What brought your sight back?"

"A lot of loving care at the hospital, I guess. It was the same kind of place as the one where you work now."

"You want to tell me what happened? Go ahead."

Lizard took a deep breath, and then she spoke. "I saw something horrible. . . . I was at home when it happened, and I saw it."

"If you don't feel comfortable talking about it, you don't have to," I told her. I could tell that she was struggling, but I didn't have a clue about what was on her mind. I had met her parents, and I knew that they were healthy and happily married. She didn't have brothers or sisters to worry about either. I'd always assumed that her childhood had been a happy one.

"I was really young at the time and, ever since, I only feel safe when I'm touching somebody. You know how little kids are—I'd get tired or scared and just want to grab something and hold tight," she said, and gave me a squeeze. "Oh, I'm sorry. Am I hurting you?"

"I'm fine. Don't worry about me. We have lots of kids at the hospital who are very clingy because they're so insecure. I understand exactly what you're talking about."

"I know you do."

Then I said it, impulsively, what I'd had on my

mind for so long. "Let's get married, Lizard. Let's find a nice place to live together."

Lizard remained silent, her face still pressed against my chest. Through the quiet, I could hear her heart beating wildly and feel the tension in her body. I was reminded of her separateness, a being with different organs, bundled in a different sheath of skin, who has dreams at night that are nothing like my own.

Then Lizard started to say something, softly, yet clearly, but stopped abruptly in midsyllable.

"I have a . . ."

Then she just lay there in silence for a few minutes. I tried to guess the rest of her sentence—"I have a . . ." What in the world did she have? A problem? A desire to be alone? A new method of birth control? A decorating tip for my apartment? I had no idea. At last, she began to speak again, her face still on my chest, and her words, as a result, a bit muffled.

"I have a confession. A secret I have to tell you."

{ { {

I used to go swimming twice a week at a health club, and it was there that I first met Lizard. She taught aerobics. Every time I saw her, I would think, Who is this woman? Unlike most of the instructors, who were bright and cheerful in the extreme, Lizard seemed somber, and of a different breed. She had narrow, upturned eyes, and a petite, tight little body. I can't say that I fell in love with her then; at first, it was more curiosity than anything.

After finishing my laps, I'd walk past the aerobics studio to find Lizard there teaching, a painfully thin figure across a sea of ample, waving bodies. She always looked like a figure in a Dalí painting, frozen in a series of absurd postures. I use the word "frozen" because she moved with such fluidity that she almost appeared to be not moving at all. No matter how loud and raucous the music, Lizard danced in a silent place, all alone.

I continued to observe her, until, one day, something happened. I'd just finished swimming and was on my way back to the locker room. As usual, I glanced in at the aerobics studio, where Lizard had all the women down on their mats and was working with them on their abdominals. I paused for a moment, and it suddenly hit me how much I would miss her if I were to come one day and find someone else in her place. You see, I had just ended a long affair with a married woman—well, actually, she had walked out on me—and I felt all used up and in no mood for romance. But, quite unexpectedly, as I stood there watching Lizard, I felt something well up within me.

I can describe my feelings at that moment fairly precisely—exhilarated, like a teenager. In fact, I felt very much as I had one warm spring evening years before. I remember sitting on the subway, thinking about where I might take my date for drinks and dinner. Life seemed wonderful. When I got off the train, she was waiting for me, looking very pretty with a flowered silk scarf, the hem of her coat wrapped neatly around her lovely legs, and a dazzling smile. I felt purified, the way you do when you look at a beautiful landscape. I didn't even care whether I got laid that night. Just seeing her was enough to satisfy me. And when I set my eyes on Lizard that day, the giddy feeling came back again, like the heady scent of spring flowers long ago.

But, what do you know, just as I was turning to leave, I heard a scream. I spun around and saw one of the students clutching at her foot, as if she'd sprained it. In the blink of an eye, Lizard was at her side. She put her hand on the woman's leg and started massaging it, looking for all the world like a doctor. The music blared on in the dimly lit studio as Lizard worked her magic. That moment seemed to last forever and Lizard appeared to me a splendid piece of sculpture, glowing among the shadows.

The woman began smiling, and Lizard grinned back, her lips a deep red. From where I stood, I couldn't really hear their conversation, so I could only guess what was happening. Lizard started to get up, and that's when I saw it—the tiny tattoo of a lizard on the inner thigh of her right leg. From that moment I knew that I wanted to be with her. That was the beginning of my strange romance with Lizard.

{ { {

Sometimes I get very burnt out at work. Even though I feel tremendous empathy for my patients, I have to force myself to remain objective. My patients focus every ounce of their energy on getting me to share their feelings, acquainting me with every nuance of their anger and pain. Yet I must remain calm, detached. It's a little like trying to ignore a plate of delicious food when you're really hungry. When it beckons you, there's no problem with enjoying the aroma and appreciating it with your eyes, but at some point you have to separate yourself and realize, like a professional waiter does, that it's not your own. It's my job to ignore those plates heaped with delicious morsels and just carry them where they need to go.

I always try to concentrate on my goal: helping my clients to get better. If I pace myself, I'm able to maintain my objectivity. I realize that this type of self-discipline is an essential skill in my line of work, because the patients, naturally, can offer no assistance. But I have a hard time when there's something on my mind, as there was that day.

I was at the same noodle shop I went to every day, eating my lunch and wondering what Lizard's secret might be. Maybe she just didn't want to marry me?

I liked this particular restaurant because it wasn't too close to the hospital, and I didn't run the risk of bumping into any of my patients there. Outside, the lush green of the park across the way glowed in the bright afternoon sun. Businessmen and retired people sat on the benches, enjoying the warm air, looking perfectly put together, perfectly uniform, and somehow beautiful; all splendid pieces of work, the men and the women, young and old. It made me remember why I did the work I did in the first place, and why I found it satisfying. I would carry on. I was all right. I knew that Lizard was at work that day with the same thoughts, beneath the same sky.

{ { {

The first time I invited Lizard out to eat was that night after I'd seen her work magic on the student. She emerged from the locker room in plain jeans and a black sweater. I had never seen her in street clothes before. Without her leotard, Lizard looked more or less like a lot of other girls, hiding herself under folds of cloth.

Lizard didn't bother to cover her mouth demurely when she laughed. Her cheeks were dotted with freckles, and she wore too much makeup. But I didn't care. Even the way she walked. I loved it. I just did.

To my eyes, Lizard seemed like a woman with a mission. Whether by choice or accident, she carried a heavy burden, and did so in earnest. I'm not sure why I felt that about her. I know that I liked her seriousness. So when she smiled so broadly, it meant something. Lizard knew how to smile.

We had dinner in a small, traditional Japanese restaurant. There were no other customers, so we sat there in the silence, facing each other. I had never been so nervous in my entire life. Lizard hardly said a word. She ate very little, and barely touched her cup of sake.

When I told her that I thought she was a good teacher, she replied, "It's fun, but I'm going to quit teaching next month."

Surprised, I asked her why.

"I have other things that I want to do."

"Like what? I know that it's none of my business, but you're so good at teaching. It seems a shame."

"I don't mind you asking. I'm going to study acupuncture."

This surprised me even more. "Acupuncture?"

"Actually, I'm better at healing than aerobics. I'm pretty good at sensing the source of people's illnesses."

"You can do that?"

"Yep."

We were eating dessert when she said philosoph-ically, "Aerobic dancing is fine as a means of expressing yourself physically, but I've come to realize that you also have to find some way to express what's inside, or you'll never really be satisfied. I mean, I've managed to survive this long by keeping myself physically active, but I know that there must be a better way. Plus, I'm already thirty-three."

"You're thirty-three?" She looked about twenty-five to me.

"Yeah, I bet I'm older than you," she said with a smile.

After dinner, we walked to the station together.

"Thanks for dinner," Lizard said. "I haven't talked about myself like this for a long time. You see, I don't really have any friends and I hardly ever see my parents. I talked too much tonight, didn't I? I'm sorry."

The dark of the night, people passing by, the wind, windows of the tall buildings, the faint sound of the warning bell that signals a train departure. Lizard's calm expression, and those dark eyes.

"I want to see you again," I said, and reached out to hold her hand in mine.

Oh God, please let me touch her hand. I'll do anything. I wanted her so badly, I thought I'd lose my mind. So I did it. I touched her hand. I just had to.

That was really how I felt at that moment. Our beginning was not a casual one, like when you just happen to feel attracted to a girl, and end up making a date with her, and then it gets dark, you have dinner together, a few drinks, and you look at each other and say, "What should we do next?" and you just know that you can probably have sex with her that very night. With Lizard, I felt overwhelmed by the desire to touch her skin, to kiss her, hold her, make love to her, no matter how it happened, I just had to have her, Lizard and no one else. Right then and there. Tears came to my eyes, I wanted her so much.

"Yes, I'd like that," she said and gave me her phone number.

She climbed the stairs to the station without looking back and was swallowed up in a wave of people. She was gone. I felt as if the world had come to an end. I felt lost without her.

{ { {

Lizard did go back to school to earn a license so that she could practice acupuncture. She even spent six months in China as an apprentice to an Oriental healer. When she returned to Japan, she opened her own clinic. It was small, but very successful, and after a short time she was able to hire someone to help her in the office.

Every day, people came from all over the country to see her. Many of them, seriously ill, had heard about Lizard by word-of-mouth and saw her as their last hope. But no matter how busy she became, her healing powers never failed. I noticed, though, that she was quieter than ever.

Once, I became curious and decided to drop by her office. I was surprised to find that it was merely a small space in an apartment building, with just one bed. It was drab and looked nothing like what you'd expect of a doctor's office.

But Lizard didn't mind, and she went quietly about her business. I found it very odd. Her bedside manner was nothing to speak of, and she had few words for her patients. I suppose that was why people who weren't seriously ill stopped coming after a visit or two. The patients whom other doctors had given up on were the ones who stayed with Lizard. After she had freed them from their pain and fear, they'd look at her adoringly, tears welling up in their eyes. When patients who had been unable to walk came out of her office on their own two feet, leaning on Lizard's arm, their waiting families would weep with joy. But Lizard just smiled and went on to the next case.

She was totally devoted to her work. Her sole purpose was helping the sick, and she didn't give a damn whether they liked her or not, or whether they showed their appreciation properly. She wanted to use her gift to help others. This moved me tremendously, and I felt proud of Lizard. At the same time, I felt slightly ashamed of myself, and wished that I could be more like her.

That evening I went home and waited for Lizard. She called and said that she'd come over at eight.

"Let's have pizza for dinner. Why don't you order that kind with the spicy sauce?"

Lizard preferred getting food delivered to going out to eat. She told me that she didn't have an aversion to people per se, but simply didn't want to see anyone else after hours. I knew how she felt. When you work with people all day, as we both did, it wears you out. And so most of the time when we were at home, we'd keep the lights low, and not even talk that much. Often, we'd put on some music and just hang out. It was an odd relationship.

Eight-thirty came and went, and Lizard still hadn't appeared. I went ahead and had some pizza and beer alone, but soon started wondering what was going on. Maybe she wasn't coming at all, ever again. She had been on the verge of confessing something to me, and then I had upset her by asking her to marry me. I knew her well enough to guess that if she wanted to break up with me, she'd just stop coming.

Yes, we weren't passionate the way we had been in the beginning, but that wasn't the point. I wanted her to be with me. I felt sad. Obviously, in our relationship, there was not much fun to be found. To be frank, I sometimes felt tempted by the nurses at the hospital, but none of them had what my Lizard had.

By eleven o'clock, I was feeling pretty drunk and hopeless, but then I heard the door swing open.

"Sorry I'm late."

She threw her arms around me. I could smell the wind in her hair.

"I didn't think you were coming," I said, calmly. (In my younger days, I might have thrown a tantrum.)

"I felt confused," Lizard said, and she sat down and started nibbling on the cold pizza.

"Want me to warm that up for you?"

"No, thanks. I'll eat it like this," she said. "You know that you're the only person I can really talk to, don't you."

"I'm aware of that. You do some talking with your patients, though, right? It's nothing to be concerned about."

"But there's something that I haven't told you. It's important."

"I'm listening."

She didn't say anything, but instead just stared into space and took a deep breath. Her profile stood out in sharp relief against the white wall. She seemed like a creature of a different species, one who lives quietly in the dark.

"Remember when I told you about losing my eyesight?"

Ghosts from her childhood. I had guessed right.

"When I was five years old, a crazy man burst into our house—he came right in through the back door—and started screaming something. He picked up a kitchen knife and stabbed my mother in the arms and thighs. And then he ran away. I was so shocked, I didn't know what to do, but somehow I managed to call my father at work. He told me to stay there with Mom until he got an ambulance.

"I could see that she was bleeding to death, and I got so scared. I tried to stop the bleeding myself by covering her wounds with my hands. That's when I discovered that I had the ability to heal. I mean, it wasn't like in the movies, like when the blood stops instantly and the wounds disappear or anything, but I could feel my hands shining. And I could feel with my hands that the blood wasn't pouring out so quickly anymore.

"By the time the ambulance arrived, I was covered with blood too, so they took both of us to the hospital. My dad finally got there, and the police, too, but somehow I couldn't speak. The doctor told us it was a miracle that the bleeding had suddenly stopped and she was still alive. That's what he said—that it was totally amazing."

I didn't say anything, but I recalled that Lizard's mother did limp a bit when she walked, and that her right leg seemed to bother her when she put weight on it.

"Mom was in a state of shock for a while after that. I lost my eyesight, and Dad became compulsive about keeping the house locked up. It was a nightmare. But after a while, my sight came back, Mom started going out by herself, shopping and stuff, and Dad could actually leave home without checking all seven locks he'd installed. But it took years before things really returned to normal.

"It was a really awful time, but I learned something important about life. Up until then, Mom had been my whole world. Even though she'd fight with Dad sometimes, to me she always acted like the perfect parent, and was very stable. But when I saw her screaming and crying, and running, and falling down, blood gushing out all over, I saw her as something else, a body losing its soul, a physical object. I realized then that the body is like a container, and that you can fix it, like you fix a car.

"Did you know that when I see people on the street, I can tell what's wrong with them? To me, people who are close to death have a darkness about them. If someone's liver is bad, it looks black to me. I can see things like that—in fact, I see too much. I started teaching aerobic dancing to keep from losing my mind. But since I met you, I've found some balance in my life. I'm dedicated to my work, and that makes me happy. It's my calling in life. I'm satisfied."

"So it's a story with a happy ending then. I don't understand what has you so upset."

"That's not all. I haven't told you the most important part yet," Lizard said. "It's something I haven't even told my parents."

She stopped talking for what seemed like a very long time, and instead sat munching on the cold pizza. I looked over and, to my great surprise, saw tears streaming down her cheeks. I had never, ever, seen Lizard cry before. Only then did I realize how devastated she was.

"So, what happened to the man who attacked your mother? Did they arrest him?" I asked.

She looked up at me blankly. I now know that if I hadn't asked that question at that very moment, I would have lost Lizard. But I did, because I loved her and I didn't want to lose her. I'm sure that's why.

"Yeah, they arrested him. After a while, he seemed

to have stabilized mentally, so they let him out," she said, her voice muffled with tears. "And then I killed him."

"What?" I said, astonished. "You did what?"

"I put a curse on him and killed him. You don't believe me, do you? It's true. I willed his death with a curse."

"I didn't know that was possible," I said. "But how?"

I had never seen Lizard talk with such animation and at such length.

"Every day I prayed that he would be hit by a car. I prayed every time something bad happened at home. And then one evening, I was sitting at home, facing the sunset, and I knew that my wish would come true. I knew for sure that he would die. And I also felt certain that I would get my sight back. About a week later I heard on the news that the man had had a breakdown and thrown himself in the path of an oncoming truck, and I thought, I did that to him. I wanted him to burn in hell.

"But when I was a little older, I started to realize just what I'd done. It horrifies me to think that no matter how many people I help, the fact will remain that I murdered a man. I've thought about that a lot since I met you—that if I have a grudge against someone, I have the power to kill him.

"To be perfectly honest, at the time, I was pleased with what I'd done. I want you to know that about me. But this is real—it's not like in the old romances about vendettas. How could I have killed a man like that? He didn't want to die. It's not like samurai days, when you could murder someone with complete impunity.

"Now I'm sure that it will come back to haunt me some day. I'll pay for it. At first, I didn't care what happened to me, I was so angry about Mom. But things have changed completely now. Mom and Dad are living happily ever after. I have my work; and now I'm with you. I just couldn't imagine that things would ever get better. It was horrible, being shut up in that house, with everyone so raw and in such pain. It felt like we were trapped in that darkness forever. I wasn't afraid of placing a curse on someone back then, because I thought I had nothing to lose. So what if it came back to haunt me? I didn't give a damn.

"But I don't feel that way anymore. I'm afraid. Everyone else has got past it, but I still have nightmares about the man. I hear his voice saying, 'I didn't kill anyone. What right did you have to take my life?' It's the truth. I'm so scared."

I could easily have told her then that his death was a coincidence, that it wasn't her fault, but as long as she felt convinced of her powers, there was nothing I could say to make it any less real. I knew that because I'd seen several kids take their own lives because they were overwhelmed by their own guilt. One girl hanged herself after letting a plant die. Another slit her wrists after forgetting to say her prayers when she was supposed to.

The better Lizard got at her job, the more she gave to others, the more she struggled. Her burden grew heavier by the day. This type of guilt is so fundamental, like sexual desire or bodily functions, that no one can share it. Many people kill themselves or others over such feelings of despair.

I have always felt frustrated by my inability to help people in this state of mind. I knew exactly what was happening to them, but there was absolutely nothing I could do. I started feeling helpless, good for nothing.

But I was glad that Lizard had told me her secret.

"Let's go out," I said, but she frowned at me. "Don't worry, I won't take you anyplace you don't want to go. It's just hard to talk here."

Lizard smiled and said, "Oh, I get it. You're going to take me to your hospital and show me all those kids who are in a lot worse shape than me, and tell me that things aren't so bad after all. Hang in there, right?"

She slipped on her light coat.

"Well, I hadn't thought of that, but if you insist," I replied jokingly.

I liked just watching Lizard—the way she threw her coat over her shoulders, the way she bowed her head when she crouched down to tie her shoes, the way her eyes glittered in the mirror when she took a peek at herself. I loved watching Lizard in her different poses. The cells of her body dying and coming into being, the curve of her cheeks, the white half-moons on her fingernails. I felt her brimming with the fluid of life, flowing with the universe. Her every gesture, every move, brought life to me, a man who had been dormant for so long.

{ { {

Outside, it smelled like early summer. The strong, silent odor of the grass filled my nostrils.

"Where are we going?" Lizard asked.

"We hardly ever go out together, do we?"

"We're both so busy."

It suddenly struck me that this might be the last phase of our relationship. There was nothing more for us to do. All the possibilities for growth seemed to be closed off to us. Like plants in a greenhouse, we depended on each other, but neither of us enjoyed the feelings of release or openness that one would wish from such a relationship. We just sat together in the dark, licking each other's wounds, and clinging together for warmth, like an old couple. I was taken aback by this realization.

Then Lizard said something, out of the blue. Her timing was magical, and it changed everything. She spoke so happily, with words full of life, full of the joy of life.

"I know. Why don't we go to the temple in Narita tonight?"

"What? You mean right now?"

"Yeah. I think it'd be fun. It's only about an hour

from here by taxi. We could be back in time for work tomorrow afternoon."

"Why Narita, of all places?"

"I don't know. I've been there before and just feel like going again. In the morning, we can get up and go buy souvenirs in those little shops by the temple, rice crackers and stuff. Let's do it."

She looked straight at me, her eyes wide.

This type of expression of desire is significant, the doctor in me thought, but more than anything I felt happy that Lizard had told me what she wanted to do. She had shared that with *me*.

"Okay. I'm with you."

We were headed for a place we both wanted to go, the two of us.

{ { {

By the time we reached Narita, it was almost one in the morning. We were lucky to find an inn with a vacancy.

Together we walked up the dark, winding road leading to the temple. The buildings along the narrow street were old and smelled of wood. The wind blew fiercely, and when we glanced up, we saw stars shining brightly in the black sky, high above the rooftops. In the wind Lizard's hair danced and fluttered around her face.

The temple gate was closed, but we could see the Sanskrit letters on the giant paper lantern at the gate and the outline of souvenir shops along the way. We were the only ones out, and I wasn't used to the silence. Lizard smiled and said that it reminded her of a ghost town.

We leaned up against the temple gate and made a bet. Would anyone walk by in the next five minutes? We waited, but no one came. Only the wind blowing up that old street, rushing past us like the sound of crowds on their way to the temple.

Lizard looked like a figure in a dream to me, standing there in the dark with her white teeth and white blouse.

"I have a confession to make, too," I said to her. "I'm not my parents' real son."

Lizard didn't say anything, nor did she look my way, but I could tell that she was there for me.

"My mother was going out with my father's

younger brother, but she broke up with him and married Dad. But Dad's brother held a terrible grudge, and it made him crazy. One day he forced his way into our house, and tied up both of my parents. He raped my mother right there in front of my dad. As if that weren't enough, he poured kerosene all over himself and lit a match. Luckily, some of the neighbors heard their screams. They saved my parents, but my mother ended up pregnant."

"That's awful. That's even worse than what happened to my family," Lizard said.

"Yeah. Dad wanted my mother to have the baby—me, that is—so she did, but then she had a breakdown, and I was taken in by relatives. I didn't live with my parents again until I was five. And then my mother committed suicide. 'I'm sorry'—those were her last words, and I was there to hear them. The poor woman."

"So your present mother is . . . ?"

"My father remarried after a while."

"I see."

"It's amazing how differently people respond to

trauma. Your mom had something awful happen to her, but now she's fine. My mother ended up taking her own life. And families are all different too—some come through it, and others don't. I wonder if it's more the personalities involved or the nature of the trauma. Either way, the children pay for it the rest of their lives. I witnessed my own mother's death, for God's sake, and that's not something I'm going to forget, ever. But at least I'm still alive, and I can enjoy a good meal now and then, and feel happy when the weather's good. I don't know."

"Is that why you became a doctor?"

"Yeah, I guess that was part of it."

I became a doctor because of that encounter with death at a tender age. It fascinated me, and even now I couldn't shake it.

And now all these confessions about the past. I actually found it shocking to realize what the two of us had been through. Our mutual attraction suddenly made sense and seemed inevitable.

"But you have to draw the line somewhere. Horrible things are happening all the time. Come on, Lizard, let's just find someplace to live together, an apartment with a nice view, or something. I think we'd work well together."

"Have you ever read a story called 'Brief Friday'?" she asked.

"No. Never heard of it."

"It's about the death of a devout Jewish couple. One night, after they've spent a pleasant day together, they get into bed, not realizing that they've accidentally left on the gas in the kitchen—they had been making a meal for the Sabbath the next day. Their bedroom fills with fumes, and by the time they realize what's happening, it's too late. But they accept it and die happy."

"I'd like to read it."

"That's the way I want to go. I don't want to see anyone else die. I just want to be content when I die, like the couple in that story."

"You and I shouldn't be thinking of things like this. We're still young, Lizard, we should have some fun. We've done our time. If we keep living this way, we might as well be dead, because we're not really living. It doesn't matter what we've been through."

Lizard nodded, even though I could tell that she

was still feeling torn apart inside. I was ecstatic. When I'm with her, I feel just like a sixteen-year-old, proud to tell all the other guys that she's my girl.

{ { {

We made our way to the old inn and lay down, exhausted. As always, Lizard buried her face in my chest and was trying to get to sleep. I felt very drowsy, and was dozing off when I heard the sound of her voice. I couldn't quite make out what she was saying.

"What's that?"

"I just wish there were someone, like God or somebody, who was in charge of what went on in this world, someone to watch over us and tell us, This type of behavior is not acceptable, or You're doing fine, or whatever. I wish someone would put a stop to all this. But there is no higher power, so we have to do it ourselves.

"Even when bizarre things happen to people around us, we just have to believe that anything is possible. At this very moment, how many people do you think are suffering? Sickness, death, betrayal—and all the violence. Think about it, how many people there are like that, right now. I wish someone would just make it stop, so there'd be less suffering."

Her sad prayer hung in the damp, dark air of the tatami room, like a melancholy poem. Half asleep, I thought about how different that dim street leading to the temple would look in the morning, crowded with people, the shops open for business, the temple gates open for all to pass through. A completely different place. I wanted to enjoy it with Lizard, take in the smells of grilled eel and roasted rice crackers, pick up a couple packages of Chinese herbal medicine and go to the temple. We could buy souvenirs to decorate our new apartment, and after that just sit and watch people go by, as the empty street comes alive.

I was too sleepy to tell her my thoughts, but I resolved to talk with her in the morning.

All this talk about death. Death. Not having her with me, no more words exchanged. Her nose pressed hard into my chest, and the place deep inside her that gave her strength, and her desire to be close to me— they would all be gone. Her silky hair, and the stray eyelash on her cheek. Her neatly painted nails, and the small burn scar on her hand. And the turn of her soul that brings all of that into existence. I wanted to talk about these things with her, everything. As long as we continue to live, I can tell her tomorrow.

Just then, I heard Lizard whisper, "Good night."

I opened my eyes, a bit surprised. I'd thought she was already asleep. Looking down I could see that her eyes were shut.

"Good night, my love."

She said sleepily, her eyes still closed, "I bet I'll go to hell when I die."

"You worry too much."

"I'm not worrying," Lizard protested. "I was thinking that I'd probably like it even better in hell because there's bound to be lots more sick people for me to heal."

And with that she fell asleep, her face like a little girl's, breathing softly. I watched her for a while and cried for several minutes, mourning our childhoods.

HELIX

I make my living as a writer, but I had a terrible hangover that day and hadn't done a bit of work the whole afternoon. I was supposed to be working on a rush job, finishing up the captions for a volume of photographs by an artist I knew. My throbbing head, though, left me totally uninterested in her pictures of crashing ocean waves.

I'm fond of collaborating with artists whose work I like, but sometimes I get the strangest feeling, almost as if we're peeking inside each other's brains, saying, Hey, do you remember that promise we made?

But that day, I hadn't promised anyone anything, or at least I was acting as though I hadn't. I just lay there in bed, staring at the clear blue autumn sky. It looked so impossibly clear that I somehow felt betrayed.

From next door, I could hear a little girl practicing the violin, and the screeching brought tears to my eyes. The tones, as she clumsily drew her bow across the strings, spread through the blue sky filling my mind. The more wrong notes she hit, the worse she sounded, the more the sound perfectly matched the shade of brilliant blue, which I could see even with my eyes shut.

As I listened, the image of the blue sky faded into another image, that of the eyelashes of a woman friend of mine. When she was at a loss for words, she would always stammer—"Uh, you know"—while, at the same time, closing her eyes. I could then see the fringe of her jet black eyelashes below the white half-moons of her eyelids, and recognize a mix of anxiety and calm in her ever-so-slightly wrinkled brow. I had the unusual sensation of having grasped her entire personality in that single expression.

Those moments of comprehension always trouble me. I feel as if my heart will stop beating, because once I know that much about a woman, it can never work out between us. And with that particular girlfriend, I was further alarmed by the way she closed her eyes like that. She screwed them shut and searched for just the right word, and finally (in fact, it probably didn't take more than a second or two), her eyes would open up wide, and she'd be her usual lucid self again. She'd say something like "Understanding is a wonderful thing."

You can't get much more straightforward than that, I'd think, but I didn't hold it against her. In fact, I considered her simplicity a great merit, and despaired my lack of similar virtues.

She called that day and said she wanted to see me. I agreed, but privately felt a bit annoyed, because I knew she had something on her mind, and was probably planning to spill her guts to me that night.

On the phone, she said, "I'll be at our favorite spot at nine." I knew, in fact, that the place she had chosen closed at eight. She was always messing with my mind.

I called to tell her that I couldn't make it, but her answering machine pleasantly reminded me that she was nowhere to be found. I had no idea where she'd be when she wasn't at work. So I had no choice but to get out of bed and go meet her.

There was not a soul on the dark streets, save the autumn wind. I encountered this emptiness at every moonlit corner I turned. Considering how clear and brisk the air was, time had slowed down drastically, but at least the cool wind purged my mind of aimless thoughts.

When I reached the cafe, it was indeed closed, and she was nowhere to be seen. A boutique of imported goods occupied half of the shop, and then there was an area by the front window with a few tables, where you could sit and get something to drink.

I liked places like that where one thing runs into another, blurring the boundaries. Night and day; the sauce on a plate; the things they're selling in the shop right up near the cafe tables. I think that came from my love for her. She was like an evening moon, her white light almost swallowed up by the gradations of pale blue sky.

I decided to go see whether she was waiting in the entranceway by the stairs leading up to the shop, but she wasn't there either. Just then, I heard her voice, oddly muffled, calling my name, as if she were speaking from the clouds far above.

I looked up and there she stood, just inside the window of the boutique. The white chairs and tables floated up in the darkness behind her. She smiled and motioned for me to join her. I climbed the stairs and found her holding the heavy glass door open for me.

"How did you get in?" I asked.

"The manager lent me the key."

She led me inside. It felt somewhat like being in a museum, with objects on display, and our footsteps and voices echoing through the space. It seemed like a completely different place from the cafe where we always met, but it wasn't. Like ghosts of the daytime crowd, we crept in and found ourselves a table.

She went over to the counter and found some clean glasses and a bottle of apple juice in the refrigerator.

"Are you allowed to raid the refrigerator, too?" I asked.

"Sure, she told me to help myself," she answered from the other side of the counter.

"Can't we turn the lights on?" I asked, a bit uneasy in the darkness.

"Oh, no. People would think the store was open and start coming in. Then what would we do?"

"I guess you're right. So we'll just sit here in the dark."

"Oh, I like it. Don't you think it's kind of fun?" she exclaimed, setting the glasses of apple juice on a tray, just like a waitress.

"Don't you have any beer?"

"But you've got a hangover, so I thought you wouldn't want any."

"How did you know?" I asked with surprise. "I don't remember telling you."

"Yes, you did, on the message on my answering machine," she said, giggling. I felt relieved.

"It's after nine at night, for heaven's sake. I feel fine."

"Whatever you want," she said, and went over to the refrigerator to get a bottle of beer.

I could tell that something was up, though I didn't know what. She was a bit too cheerful, and the sound of her footsteps as she had walked over to get the beer sounded like someone leaving. That made me nervous.

Plus, I was having a hard time enjoying my beer in that dark room. I felt for all the world like I was having a drink at the North Pole, sparkling with ice and frigid. Maybe it was the alcohol in my body from the night before, or the dim moonscape of the cafe, but I felt a buzz before I finished the first glass.

"I wanted to tell you about this seminar I'm going to next week," she said.

"What kind of seminar?"

"One of my girlfriend's having some personal problems, and then someone told her about this seminar. It's supposed to be really radical, so she wanted me to go with her."

"Radical? What's that supposed to mean?"

"She said that they completely clear your mind. It's not one of those mental development things or meditation. They take you down to zero, so you can start all over again. They told her that most of the thoughts and memories crowding our minds are totally unnecessary. Doesn't that sound good?"

"No, it sounds awful. And besides, who decides what is necessary and what isn't?"

"I guess that's the chance you take if you go to one of these sessions. You might even end up forgetting things that seemed really important to you, things you don't want to forget."

"Like stuff you're obsessing about?"

"That, too. My girlfriend is really depressed about her divorce, and I think that's what she wants to forget. I bet she won't be able to, though."

"Don't go," I told her, insistently.

"But I can't let her go by herself. She's counting on me," she said. "And, besides, I want to see what it's like. How can I tell if it's right for her if I don't go myself?"

"I don't trust those kinds of places. Who wants to forget everything anyway?"

"It's okay to get rid of your bad memories, don't you think? What's wrong with that?"

"But you can do that on your own. At least then you get to choose what you forget, right?"

She closed her eyes and searched for the right words. Then she opened her eyes and said, "Well, no matter what happens, I know that I won't forget you."

"How do you know you won't?"

"I just do. Don't get so uptight," she said with a grin. I knew full well that privately, deep inside, she was worried. I could almost hear her voice.

"I'd like to forget about the part of me who wants to forget you."

I knew that there was no more point in trying to talk her out of it. I was bummed.

"You might forget all about our relationship, for all I know," I said, grinning.

"All thousand years of it?" she asked, also with a smile. Sometimes when she'd say something like that, it seemed real. Just for an instant, but still, very true. Maybe it was the cheerful, deep sound of her voice—I could almost believe that we'd been together for a thousand years.

"Do you think I'd forget the first time we went on a trip together?"

"We were so young then. Nineteen."

"Yeah, remember how the maid at that inn said to me, 'Your wife is so young!'? I can't believe how people stick their noses into other people's business!"

"Yeah, especially since I wasn't any older than you."

"No, but you looked older. Remember how big that room was? It was so spooky. Yeah, full of dark shadows."

"But then we went out into the garden, and looked at the stars. I couldn't believe how bright they were."

"The grass smelled so fresh. That's one of the things I love about summer."

"You had your hair cut short then."

"And we put our futons right next to each other."

"Yeah."

"Then you kept telling me ghost stories, and I got too scared to go to the spa alone."

"So I went with you."

"And we made love in that mineral bath outside, near the garden."

"Right, it was like doing it in a jungle."

"The stars were gorgeous. . . . That was so much fun, wasn't it?"

"It would be like dying."

"What are you talking about?"

"If you lost your memory."

"Oh, stop being so morose."

"Maybe they do something to you like in *One Flew over the Cuckoo's Nest.*"

"Like a lobotomy? Are you kidding? Of course not." She shut her eyes. "They just make you forget memories you don't need anymore."

"Like me?"

"No! But, you know, to tell you the truth, I'm not sure which ones are necessary and which aren't."

"Let's get out of here. It's too quiet. I feel like I'm at a summit conference or something."

"Yeah, doesn't the echo in here make you feel like you're saying something profound? Wait a sec. I want to check out the store."

We strolled around, glancing at the imported items on the glass display shelves. The crystal glasses, stacked one on top of another, sparkled like prisms, looking much more elegant than in broad daylight.

We went out the front door, and locked it, just as if we were leaving our own apartment. Outside, we were greeted by a gust of cold wind, and, with that, the clock started ticking once again.

"Let's have a drink somewhere before we go home."

"Good idea." I was feeling a lot happier.

{ { {

"I promise that I'll be able to recover all my memories of you," she said, all of a sudden, as we were walking along. "Even if I forget them at first."

"Every single one?"

"Of course. We've done so much together, wherever I go and whatever I see, I think of you. Newborn babies; the pattern on the plate that you can see under a paper-thin slice of sashimi; fireworks in August. The moon hidden behind clouds over the ocean at night. When I'm sitting down someplace, inadvertently step on someone's toes, and have to apologize. And when someone picks up something I've dropped, and I thank him. When I see an elderly man tottering along, and wonder how much longer he has to live. Dogs and cats peeking out from alleyways. A beautiful view from a tall building. The warm blast of air you feel when you go down into a subway station. The phone ringing in the middle of the night. Even when I have crushes on other men, I always see you in the curve of their eyebrows."

"So, does that mean every single thing on earth reminds you of me?"

Once again, she closed her eyes, and then, opening them, looked directly at me, her eyes shining like glass.

"No, just everything in my heart."

"So, you mean, your love for me?" I said, somewhat surprised.

At that moment, I saw a bright flash and, a split second later, heard a loud rumble, like thunder. At first

I didn't know what had happened. We looked up and saw a glow from the top of the building across the way, and then flames flared up. And there was a dull boom, accompanied by splinters of glass raining down in slow motion through the darkness.

In a matter of seconds, people, awakened from sleep by the noise, started pouring into the street from every doorway. Over the din of voices, we could hear ambulances and police cars approaching the scene, sirens wailing.

"It must have been a bomb!" I said, excited by the spectacle.

"And we were the only witnesses, don't you think? I hope no one got hurt."

"I doubt it. It's an office building, and there weren't any lights on. Besides, we were the only people on the street. I bet it was just some kids."

"I hope so. It looked really pretty, though, didn't it? This might sound silly, but it looked like fireworks to me."

"Yeah, I've never seen anything like it."

"Fantastic."

She looked up toward the sky again. I gazed at her profile, and thought about the two of us.

{ { {

Your love is different from mine. What I mean is, when you close your eyes, for that moment, the center of the universe comes to reside within you. And you become a small figure within that vastness, which spreads without limit behind you, and continues to expand at tremendous speed, to engulf all of my past, even before I was born, and every word I've ever written, and each view I've seen, and all the constellations, and the darkness of outer space that surrounds the small blue ball that is earth. Then, when you open your eyes, all that disappears.

I anticipate the next time you are troubled and must close your eyes again.

The way we think may be completely different, but you and I are an ancient, archetypal couple, the original man and woman. We are the model for Adam and Eve. For all couples in love, there comes a moment when a man gazes at a woman with the very same kind of realization. It is an infinite helix, the dance of two souls resonating, like the twist of DNA, like the vast universe.

Oddly, at that moment, she looked over at me and smiled. As if in response to what I'd been thinking, she said, "That was beautiful. I'll never forget it."

DREAMING OF
KIMCHEE

In just about every women's magazine you pick up, you'll find an article about extramarital affairs. The contents don't vary much:

> Keep in mind that married men who have extramarital affairs rarely leave their wives to marry their lovers. If you can cope with that reality, then an affair with a married man may be just the thing for you. A woman is wise to regard such relationships as temporary, and something to learn from, rather than hoping for something more permanent.

I read dozens of those articles, but never took them to heart.

I didn't ransack the magazine stands trying to find magazines with "men who cheat on their wives" articles. I just liked buying a magazine on the way home from work when I knew I would have enough time to read it, on the rare occasion when I got out of work at a decent hour. Could I help it that they always featured a "loving a married man" article?

I relished those days when I had a few hours to relax at home. I wouldn't make a big deal about dinner, because I preferred to spend my time watching TV, or writing long-overdue letters to friends. Sometimes I'd just gab on the phone for an hour or so. Later in the evening, I'd never miss my soak in a hot bath, after which I'd jump into bed, ready to read my new magazine from cover to cover, including the obligatory blurb about the difficulties of getting involved with a married man. But I really just skimmed them without paying much attention, which is hard to believe, considering.

I adored the apartment I had then—my little castle, with a decorating job by yours truly. I chose every detail down to the towels in the bathroom. I looked for ages before I found dishes that I liked. Once ensconced inside my warm, safe haven, I forgot about everything, and even tried to banish work from my mind. And I looked forward to the nightly phone call from my boyfriend, at 10:00 P.M. sharp. Waiting for his call was part of my routine, even if I was too bushed to do much else.

{ { {

I liked my life then. Those magazine articles didn't bother me at all, even the "true confession" type, which were depressing and reeked of despair. I was so unaware that I could even resist the devastating pessimism of the trained professionals. I was in control. I'd sit there in my happy home, paging through my glossy magazines, until I found yet another article on the topic. I'd skim through it coolly, as if the subject didn't apply. When I was done reading, I'd take another bite of whatever cookie I was devouring that night, flip to the next page in the magazine, and forget all about it. Very odd, now that I think about it. It depresses me to recall my emotional state then.

Even though our love was strong and constant, we had our share of disagreements. I remember once we argued on the phone, and, after I'd slammed the receiver down, I swore to myself that I'd never talk to him again. And then there was the time when I had a conversation with his wife in person—that blew me away. But the most unbelievable thing was me in my wonderful, cozy, warm little room, watching TV, and sitting there reading articles about infidelity as if all the pain and doubt and uncertainty they talked about had absolutely nothing to do with me.

I can picture myself now, like someone I'd see through a window, a woman safe in a warm asylum. I would imagine that she needed a hug, though I'm not sure why, because ultimately no one can comfort her, not her lover, not her parents, and certainly not the present me, the victor.

"You really don't want to be reading articles like that," I want to tell her. "You pretend to be strong, but I know it hurts a lot."

If there is a God, I bet She watches over us like that. Memories are energy, and if they aren't defused, they remain to haunt you. Of course God would worry, and hover around me, as I lay there leafing through my magazine, and shake me with an invisible hand.

"It's right here. Don't pretend you don't feel it," She would yell, in a silent voice.

In the end, I married my lover. He left his wife and we got married.

The moment we met, I felt certain that he and I would spend some part of our lives together. There was no way around it. I didn't intuit the inevitability of our relationship, or will it into being. I simply knew it would happen. Our relationship came about naturally, without dreams or desire.

It wasn't as easy as I'm making it sound, of course. After all, I was in love with a married man, and sometimes the stress of the relationship hurt me tremendously. I'd get so sick of the whole thing that I'd feel like giving up. Every time we'd hit a snag, I'd find myself wondering why. We'll end up together eventually, so why all this backsliding? Sometimes it didn't even seem worth it, and I would stop trying, ready to give it all up. Gradually, though, I stopped holding back and just went with the flow. There was no point in resisting, because he and I were born into this world to be together.

I found out that only 5 percent of couples like us end up getting married. I felt uncomfortable being made into a statistic like that, though, because I knew that we weren't just like every other couple.

Thinking about it now, I realize that a strange, invisible kind of pressure had taken control of me then, a pressure to conform. It's like when you go out to a restaurant with a group of friends and you plan to all split the bill evenly, you can't very well order a whole meal for yourself if everyone else is just having a cup of coffee. Just like you're obliged to go on company trips, even if you don't want to. Your superiors will look down on you if you don't. That's the way the world works.

Of course, it's natural for taxi drivers who are working late at night to look for a fare with a long trip. If a single woman goes bar hopping by herself, people conclude that she's loose. If you have lunch with a single guy from the office, the women you usually eat with get upset. All these things seem so trivial, yet the rules are hard and fast. It's weird. Just like it's strange how everyone automatically makes assumptions about people who are having affairs before they've heard the particulars. And then they feel like it's their place to judge the morality of those involved.

In my case, I promised myself that I would ignore what other people thought, and do what I needed to do for myself. And I realize now that I was waging a psychic battle with other things as well—and it wasn't just with him, his wife, and myself. It's the way society is now. You're not supposed to be by yourself. You get caught in the net, and you can feel it tugging at you as you try to get away from it, just as if you've walked into a spider's web. You struggle to free yourself, but you can't. It's in the air; there's no escape from this force, one so inferior to the life force, the energy within us. You can pretend to ignore it, but it still obscures your vision.

We'd been married for two years. We didn't have children, and I'd quit my job a year before. We had one cat and lived in a condo that we had bought together.

Every morning before he left for work, he'd promise to call if he'd be late getting home. Then he'd switch off the TV, and go. Silence filled up the apartment. My husband didn't eat breakfast, so I would usually still be in bed. I'd just lie there, quietly, watching him leave. When I heard him close the door behind him, a feeling of regret would flash through the room, and for a moment I would feel so lonesome. I could see the rays of morning sunlight shining across the dining room table and smell the coffee. The cat would wander into our bedroom, jump onto the bed, and curl up by my feet. As I gazed down at her, I'd drift off to sleep again.

At first, I wouldn't know where I was when I woke up. Sometimes I'd call my little sister's name.

"Kyon-chan? Are you there?"

During the last part of our "affair," he would come to my apartment every night. We'd eat dinner together, have a couple of beers, and then go to bed. In the morning, he'd go off to work, and all that I had left were a couple pairs of his socks and some shirts, and his pillow next to mine. Eventually, I tired of this arrangement, and asked my sister if she wanted to share an apartment with me. She loved the idea, because it meant we'd be able to afford a bigger place by pooling our money.

Partly, I made the move to test our relationship, although I didn't relish the idea of hunting for hotel rooms where we could make love. If something like this would make our love go sour, then it wasn't meant to last anyway. But everything turned out to be fine, even when I didn't have a place of my own. Our future together seemed bright.

And I felt better, too. I'd been losing weight and was feeling down, but life with my sister agreed with me. She was like an ice pack when you have a fever, or a pot of bubbling stew and a soft cozy blanket on a cold winter day. I hadn't realized how stressed out I'd been.

We got along well, my sister and I. I'd wake up in the morning to hear her filling the teapot with fresh water for tea. She'd take charge and tell me what to do, like "Get off your butt and go clean the bathroom." One of my favorite things was to buy sweets from the bakery on my way home from work, so that she and I could spend time together having tea and talking about all the things that had happened that day. She always understood what was on my mind, but never tried to second-guess me. Plus, on my days off, I no longer had to spend the evening in front of the television watching variety shows all by myself.

I was starved for that kind of ordinary companionship and routine. A relationship with a married man totally lacks those aspects, of course, because he can get his creature comforts from his wife at home, if he wants to. That's one reason extramarital affairs are better avoided.

Every morning, I'd wake up and hear my sister bustling around in the next room. I'd just lie there half asleep, thinking about her, innocently, like a child. I knew that she would never do anything to hurt me. I felt absolutely safe with her. I could drift back to sleep without a care in the world, knowing that she'd be there when I woke up, and that she, at least, didn't have another home to go to. Her place was with me. My sister loved me as much as she loved her boyfriend, though in a sisterly way, and I knew that she would never cause me pain. Not like him, even though he loved me as much as he had loved his wife.

Most days, I'd eventually fall back asleep, nestled in my warm comforter, at peace with the world. Life was good.

That's why, after he got divorced, I wasn't exactly overjoyed when he asked me to marry him. Of course it made me happy that he had proposed to me, but I was finding life with my sister very comfortable. I might not have made it if I hadn't spent that time healing and trying to feel whole again. At the same time, I realized that I couldn't live with my sister for the rest of my life, and that's why I decided to take the leap into a new existence, one fraught with difficulty.

Our relationship had started out under rocky circumstances, and marriage itself did not alleviate all of the problems. For me, this meant that I was condemned to a role of eternal waiting, a state of anticipation of the day when the fatigue and tension implicit to our love would disappear.

To give a concrete example, something very strange would happen when he'd called to let me know that he'd be home late from work. By the time he'd phoned me, I'd usually already have dinner made, but I never spent much time on cooking anyway, so it didn't bother me that he wasn't going to eat at home. In fact, I couldn't believe how considerate he was. Not only would he keep me informed of his plans, he'd say, "Instead of sitting at home by yourself, why don't you go and have dinner at your sister's?"

For a while after saying good-bye and hanging up, I'd be fine, but in less than half an hour I started to feel it, something like a chemical reaction, completely beyond my control. I would sit there staring into space, under the influence of this imperative to wait that filled the apartment like a mysterious vapor. Within a couple of hours, it had circulated throughout my body, and immobilized me completely. Eventually, I became impervious to everything around me, and couldn't respond to the sound of the telephone ringing, or recognize my books, the TV screen, the bath, anything, as if I had been enveloped in an impenetrable membrane. Only my mind was active, as all of the terrible possibilities visited me like evil spirits.

I longed for my old, simple life with my sister, when I could be myself completely. At the same time I had to remind myself that I had chosen to leave her, and to live with him as man and wife, but to no avail. I still felt just awful. What did work like a charm was chanting to myself, "This is the way life is, and I can't change it." I even tried saying it out loud, and somehow that made the clouds clear. I never spoke with my husband about it. There was no point talking. It was a really rough time for me.

{ { {

The time I met his wife, she let me know the score in no uncertain terms. She's awfully harsh, I thought, with amazing nonchalance.

"In case it's never occurred to you, men who are

unfaithful once are bound to cheat again. I promise you that's how he is. He can't resist."

Could she possibly be right? I wondered. There's nothing for us to hold on to, no one we can keep forever as our own. Our souls are simply floating, anyway, waiting to be swept along with the current.

I remember her saying to me, "I waited for him every day. Even after I found out about you, I was still waiting for him, every day, for months and months."

She would also write me letters telling me about her many days of waiting. Even though I expected some pain from loving a married man, I had not anticipated how much it would actually tear me apart. At times, I felt tremendous sympathy for her, despite my position as adversary. After all, we loved the same man.

The last time I saw her, I felt overwhelmed by the weight of her pain. All she could do the whole time was complain about what a monster he was, and how much he had hurt her, but eventually my sympathy turned to anger. I said to her, "You're obsessing. You've got to let go of him," and without hesitation she raised her hand and slapped me hard across the face. The sting brought tears to my eyes.

It was the touch of her hand that had implanted the compulsion to wait for him in me, and eventually it spread throughout my body and grew, as if I'd been possessed by an alien. It sucked away all my energy, and the gauges in my body registered near empty.

How else could it have worked? From her point of view, I (Party A) stole her (Party B's) dreams and hopes for the future. (This is B's take on the situation, by the way, not mine. I think that no one individual possesses the power to alter the natural course of things. Besides, Party B is hardly guaranteed a happy future simply by remaining with her original partner.) So all the energy that Party B had been concentrating on her own future is now focused on Party A. If that energy becomes a negative force, then something like what happened between the two of us is inevitable. At least, that's how it looked to me, ever since she put her mark on me.

I worried, as all newlyweds do, that my new husband might fall in love with someone else, just as he had fallen in love with me. Then there was the additional twist to my fears. From early on, I realized that my daily life would be plagued with such anxiety, and I tried to avoid the pain of contemplating our future together.

Long ago, people would have said that I was possessed by evil spirits; now, we label it neurotic. I was suffering under the stress of her resentment. For my part, I saw it as the inevitable result of what I did. I altered the course, changed the plot. Of course, the spin-off from that glitch came to rest on me.

When I confessed my fears to friends, they would conclude that I just wasn't accustomed to married life. "You're just exhausted from trying to learn to live with another person!" they'd say, or "It takes a long time to adjust." I admit, that was a large part of it, for me, and for him too, for that matter. He had been with his wife for a long time. Another aspect of it, I must confess, was that guilt needling at my conscience.

{ { {

Then one day, when my exhaustion was at its peak, something happened. I was taking it easy, trying to fight off a cold and a headache. He had called to tell me that he wouldn't be home in time for dinner, but then appeared at a reasonable hour anyway.

A smile on his face, he fished inside his briefcase

and pulled out a bag. Through the translucent plastic, I could see a jar with something bright orange in it.

"Look what somebody gave me!" he exclaimed.

"What is it?"

"It's kimchee, the spicy Korean pickles."

"Somebody at work brought you kimchee?" I asked curiously. He handed the bag to me, and I could smell the spicy, luscious odor of cabbage and garlic.

"Oh, sorry, I thought I'd told you. I stopped in at the office this morning, but then I went over to Mr. Endo's house and spent most of the day there. We needed some time together to discuss a design he's doing for us. Anyway, his wife made that kimchee. She's Korean, so it's the real thing."

I knew that he was probably telling me the truth. If he were that good at making up complicated lies, he could have led a double life without ever having to marry me at all. But how was I to tell? He might be lying. He could have bought the kimchee at the store, and then just torn off the price tag. I could find out easily enough by looking at the package.

But I didn't inspect the bag or its contents because I hated the thought of stooping so low. If I let myself get carried away, and gave in to paranoia, I wouldn't be able to trust myself, much less my husband or anyone else.

"Thanks," I said feebly, and, my eyes averted, shoved the bag into the refrigerator. I could barely manage that.

My headache finally went away and I tried calling my sister to chase away my blues. I even took a leisurely bath, but nothing worked. I wasn't surprised when he asked, "What's the matter? Is something bothering you?"

"No, everything's fine," I replied, but I couldn't even manage a smile. I was like a faded flower, devoid of energy.

Later that evening, we sat down together in front of the TV with some beers and a dish of kimchee to nibble on. We chatted as we watched some silly program, and, at one point, he commented that I seemed under the weather lately. I tried denying it and claimed that I was just a bit worn out, that's all.

And then something amazing happened to me. I felt so clearly that I was changing inside, at that very moment, that I glanced at my watch to check the time.

It was 10:15 P.M. To my utter astonishment, my head had cleared completely. I felt as if the fog that had been clouding my eyes had lifted. I don't know how it happened, but it occurred to me that such lucidity wasn't entirely new for me. Once, long before, I had been able to see clearly.

Or had it been that long ago? That was how I had felt when I first met him, as though I could relish each of the many flavors that life offers.

Love had given me energy and clarity of vision. Everything appeared vivid, down to the smallest detail, and I felt convinced that I could triumph over everything. To ensure my victory, and so as not to forget, I doted over every moment of our time together, and tried to absorb the details as if they were full of essential bits of information.

The bittersweet feeling of beautiful mornings when we made a date; the scent of the breeze during our brief times together; the steep slope of the street, down which we walked so fast, too fast. Glass, asphalt, mailboxes, guardrails, fingernails. The display windows of department stores; sunlight reflected off the windows of tall buildings.

Those days, everything looked beautiful to me, and good. The things around me appeared distinct, their outlines graced by a fragrant presence. I could feel the excitement, that exhilaration deep inside. When I closed my eyes, I saw waves of energy swirling about, like patterns in a marble block.

Then I began to wonder what had just happened to me. Why had I been so overtaken by these sensations? Precisely at that moment, the phone rang. My husband answered it.

The call seemed to be for him so I gathered up the empty beer bottles and carried them into the kitchen. I felt refreshed, maybe even a little happy. Something was changing inside me. I decided to celebrate with another glass of beer. As I opened the refrigerator door, it struck me that I was a very lucky woman. My future was secure, my marriage happy, and we even had our own space, a place we had chosen, just the two of us. I had the good fortune to have a roof over my head, a cozy place where I could make my bed. What on earth had been bothering me?

I could only faintly hear his side of the phone conversation from where I stood. I wondered whom he was talking with, and then felt pleasure in the fact that this question mark no longer threatened me. Earlier that same day it would have been enough to bring me down.

I'll just ask him who called. It's no big deal. Maybe jealousy is an indication of a general lack of energy, rather than of problems in the relationship itself.

I heard him say good-bye as I carried the cold bottle of beer into the living room.

"Who was it?"

And he said the name of his ex-wife.

She had never called our place before, so I felt puzzled.

"Is something wrong?"

"Listen to this one. Remember I told you that she kept telling me that it was so unfair of me to leave her at this time in her life? 'No man would want me at this age.' Well, now she says that she's found a new husband, and he's younger than she is. They've got their marriage license already, and a new apartment and everything. She said that she hadn't been planning to tell me, but then she changed her mind."

Suddenly, it all made sense to me. I know a coincidence when I see one, and this was no coincidence. Another line had converged to form a circle. Oddly, it felt so natural to me that I wasn't even surprised at how it had happened. A force, capable of liberating us from the burden of accumulated guilt, circled in to touch us that night.

"How are you doing?"

"Fine . . . relieved, actually, because now I feel like you and I can finally start our own life together," he said. "And I'm not saying that what we've had up to now hasn't been real. It's just that I couldn't stop feeling guilty about what I'd done."

"I understand."

{ { {

Later, I realized why I'd felt so heady. It wasn't just because I'd been freed of the burden of negative feelings; I'd also come down with a fever. I decided to sleep on an ice-pack pillow.

"What smells in here?" he said from his side of the bed.

"Hmmm. I bet it's the kimchee."

"So you think that we're the ones who smell, because we ate that stuff, huh?"

We both got up and sniffed about the room, trying to find the source of the smell.

"Oh, look," I said. "It's got to be my ice pack."

He laughed.

"Yeah, you could smell it in the freezer too," I said. After that, I tried wrapping a towel around the pack, but it still stunk. Even so, I needed relief from the fever, so I decided to put up with the odor. We turned the lights off, and our bedroom smelled faintly of kimchee.

When I finally dozed off, I dreamed that I was strolling through a Korean market. The dream was brief, but quite vivid. In my one hand—I thought it was empty, but then I realized that I was holding someone else's hand. I looked up and saw my husband's face. And I remember seeing the bright sun, and all the goods in the market bathed in the sunlight, and the commotion, and the smell of garlic, and women with boldly drawn arched eyebrows. Red, green, pink, blue, in dazzling bright shades.

We were there to buy some kimchee. We saw big jars and barrels full of bright red pickles. He said that he wanted some special kind of kimchee. Let's go somewhere else to buy it, he said. Over that way.

And then reality broke into my dream; I had to pee. (Too much beer!) I sat up in bed, and felt my head. I was still feverish. When I got back from the bathroom, I could see well enough in the dark room to know that he was lying there with his eyes wide open.

"Having trouble getting to sleep?" I asked.

He replied drowsily, "I just had a dream about kimchee. You and I were eating at a Korean barbecue restaurant."

"That sounds like the dream I just had!"

"That smell goes right to your brain, doesn't it?"

"Unbelievable."

We said good night, and I lay down again. It felt good putting my feverish head down on the cool pillow, scented with kimchee. As I drifted off, I thought of our common dream, and the food, the odor, and the vibes in the room that had brought it about. Despite being bound as separate physical entities, we could share these aspects of daily life, and I knew that sharing, this kind of connection, was what constituted our life together.

I thought about the complications of what I'd been dealing with lately. And then I understood that actually it wasn't just the relationship—I had so much baggage from my childhood, from before I was born into this world, too. I understood that for the first time that night. And I knew it would always be that way, until we die. Even after we're dead.

But at last I had a chance to rest, after that long period of strain. I was tired and wanted to sleep. I felt that when I woke up the next morning, I would start anew. I would breathe fresh air, and start a day of entirely new experiences. It reminded me of the feelings I used to have when I was younger, like after a big test, or the night after a major school event. I'd always looked forward to waking up the next morning, when a fresh breeze would come to sweep through me, cleansing me. And when I opened my eyes at dawn, I'd feel a glow, a radiant white pearl. I hoped, nearly prayed, for that to happen again. That night, I believed with the same purity and innocence.

BLOOD AND WATER

When I was younger, I used to think that the occult, religion, New Age, Kitaro, channeling, and all that kind of stuff was really stupid. I mean, when I'd hear people talking about it on television, it really turned me off. Totally. But then you couldn't get away from it. Every newspaper I picked up, gossip on the streets—enough is enough.

But I don't feel that way now. I guess that I feel more comfortable hearing about spirituality. Sometimes I even take it for granted, kind of like I'm not constantly aware of the blood circulating through my body. Just like I don't dwell on my nose, which I think is really ugly. I've learned to live with it.

Allow me to explain. I guess that it all goes back

to my parents. Both of them are such kind, honest people—too good for this world, like saints. But then, one day when I was a little girl, something terrible happened to them. Some guy stole all their money, every cent they had worked so hard for. The man was an old friend of my father and his business partner, and then he did something like that to them. What were they supposed to do? Say that they forgave him? Even they couldn't do that, and instead they got involved in a religious sect, one based on Esoteric Buddhism.

At first, the sect didn't even have a name. The leader was supposed to be able to read people's minds (or at least that's what they said about him), but to me he was simply a very sensitive, perceptive person. He and his followers built a village, where they all lived together. By drawing on the various talents of the believers, they were finally able to start proselytizing, like the big religious sects did.

From what I understand, the leader of the sect had approached Father on the street one day. Father was extremely impressed by his compassion and even now insists that he was given the answers to all of his questions that day—though he would never tell me exactly what the leader said to him. In the end, my parents sold their house and property, paid off all their debts, and moved to the small village founded by the leader. It happened when I was very young. I grew up in the village. In fact, I lived there for twelve years.

By the time I was eighteen, I couldn't stand it anymore, and so I ran away. It's difficult for me to explain why I needed to leave, especially since I loved my parents, and everyone else in the village was good to me. I think maybe it's something similar to people from the countryside desperately wanting to move to Tokyo, convinced that the big city will change everything for them. I'm just guessing, because I've never been in that position. I suppose that I felt pessimistic about the beliefs that kept my parents alive and happy, and the effect they had on me. At some point, it struck me that the village and my parents reeked of defeat, and that I did too. A village full of losers.

Now I can recognize that I was quite immature in my thinking then, but, at the time, nothing that my parents said, and nothing that the other believers did, in all of their wisdom, could suppress my youthful fervor. Somewhere, on the other side of those mountains, the people of my dreams existed, people whom I imagined as uncommonly beautiful, powerful beings of great substance. My imaginary men and women laughed and cried; they weren't afraid of betrayal or heartbreak. They had a sense of purpose, and wouldn't give in even to abuse. They knew what life was all about.

My people wouldn't be like the believers in the village, who typically used superficial smiles to escape uncomfortable situations. Even if the villagers couldn't stand certain people, they would still pretend to love them. It didn't matter if you had a good reason to be angry with someone, you were still expected to forgive him. I felt as if the ways of the villagers—all their nuanced kindnesses and their techniques of avoidance—were eating away at my heart.

I won't deny that I admired some of the residents, those who didn't pompously claim that they had achieved spiritual enlightenment—you know, satori and all that. A few of them impressed me as exceptionally fine people, and there were several whom I looked up to. Despite my feelings of respect for them, I knew that I could never change within the confines of the village. I would have to leave.

When I finally made it to Tokyo and got to know lots of so-called normal people there, I realized that, in any population, the proportions aren't going to differ that much. In other words, wherever you go, you're bound to run into more escapists who just can't cope than healthy people who live their lives to the fullest. Now that I think of it, I actually met more losers in Tokyo than in the village. And then there were, of course, the amazing ones in the city, too, the kind of people who'd say shocking things and make me laugh. I loved being around them. So, in the end, the big difference between the village and the outside world was not so much the kind of people, but the unique mood. Sometimes I'd wonder why I'd come to Tokyo in the first place.

In the village, the only halfway decent piece of clothing I had was a black dress Mother had bought for me. I wanted to look pretty and dress up just like any other girl, so when I got to Tokyo and saw the variety, I went nuts. The clothes didn't have to be fancy or expensive. I could still have fun with them, going wherever I wanted and thinking that I fit in and was at the height of fashion. In other words, I had found the right colors for my new "self," just like someone who's completed training in some discipline.

At first, I loved every minute of my life there and found it all so glamorous. I didn't have to be doing anything special; simply taking in my new surroundings was entertainment. The starless nights and polluted air didn't bother me. It didn't matter if I felt lousy. I spent my days walking around the city, where I fell head over heels with every site: the game centers and the discos; the parks; the bars and cafes; the trendy, hip department stores.

My parents were understanding about my move to the big city, and never tried to force me to return to the village. Instead, they responded to my move by sending me a long letter saying I should come home when and if I wanted to, along with the passbook to their savings account. My parents still had some money in the bank—it wasn't forbidden by the sect—although they scarcely had any need for cash in the village itself. So I withdrew what little remained from their earlier life and used it to pay for the deposit on my apartment.

Not long after that, my money almost gone, I found a job in a design company, thanks to a man whom I'd dated for a while, the middle-aged married man who owned the business. Though I hadn't attended regular school, I had learned lots from people in the village, like the fundamentals of design (there were lots of art school graduates there), word processing, and basic math, even the pleasures of making love in the great outdoors. Everyone in the village had time on their hands, and they were more than willing to share their knowledge with others.

So I didn't have such a hard time fitting in with people in the city, because I was fully aware of the scars my upbringing had left on me. I knew why I had left the village, and I tried to remember where I had come from and where I was trying to go.

Still, sometimes in the middle of the night, I'd wake up sobbing and thinking of Mom and Dad. Sure, I missed them a lot. And I realized how much they had sacrificed for me, but that wasn't why I was crying. It was more the realization that they would never change, and that, no matter how far I traveled on this earth, Mom and Dad would live in that small village forever, along with all the other believers, and that they'd always love me, in their own special way. In a certain sense, nothing had changed. I could go home anytime, confident that they would take me back into the fold, in that strange, gentle manner of theirs, smiling and always disarmingly cheerful. Even if it seemed fake to me, that was the kind of love that I knew best.

That's where I belong, I'd think to myself, and some nights I'd crave it so much that I'd decide to take the first train back the next morning. No one else could go home again, even if they wanted to. For lots of people, in fact, the impossibility of return only intensifies their yearning. It was possible for me, and me alone, to return to my past, those green days where time had stopped. And several times I nearly gave in to that temptation.

But I knew that I never would go back, no matter how alone or lost I felt, no matter how those feelings overwhelmed me. I knew full well how dangerous it would be for me even to visit the village. Not that I didn't want to—I wanted that more than anything in the world—but something inside stopped me. That's why I spent so many nights crying in bed, trying to resist, trying hard to stay away.

In the morning, I'd wake up and see the sunny sky

outside my window, get up, and go to work as usual. And my mind would be such a blank that I couldn't remember what had been causing me so much pain the night before. By the time I got on the train, my eyes wouldn't even be puffy and red anymore.

At the office, I was pretty popular. I admit that sometimes I'd say things that showed how out of the loop I was, and my officemates would laugh at me— "You're right out of the Stone Age," they'd say. But mostly I hung out like everyone else. I had my share of boys who liked me, and people who picked on me and bossed me around. I also had friends who shared their secrets and gave me presents on my birthday. Life continued that way, calm and uneventful, for about two years.

And then I met Akira and discovered why I had come to Tokyo. Not long after, we started living together.

He didn't have a job, but instead stayed at home and made these metal and wood objects, about the size of your palm. I don't know exactly how to describe the shape. They're not accessories or jewelry or anything like that.

For tools, he uses some pliers, and chisels, and then he kind of bends the metal, you know, kind of like those spoons you see with the curved handles. I'm not sure exactly how he does it, but anyway, maybe you get the idea.

Along with my job at the design firm, I sold Akira's things on the side. Even though it was all very small scale and word of mouth, Akira didn't like dealing with people at all, so I did it for him.

{ { {

Judging from the voice on the phone, our customer that day was a woman in her late twenties. I told Akira that I was going out to meet her, and he saw me to the door. She and I had arranged to meet in a cafe in one of the skyscrapers in Shinjuku, and I said that I would be wearing a red skirt.

She had no trouble finding me. She was an attractive woman with sharp features and wore a tailored jacket and skirt. She looked me straight in the eye and smiled as she came up to greet me.

I just said hello. I didn't tell her my name or give

her a business card. Akira thought that advertising was too much of a bother.

"Hello, I'm Ms. Okubo," she said cheerfully.

"Nice to meet you. Please make yourself comfortable," I said, and pulled out a package wrapped in light brown paper from my bag. It made a solid thump when I set it down on the table.

"May I have a look?" she asked, reaching out with childlike glee. Since most of our customers are solid, honest people like her, I never have to worry.

"Please do."

She pulled open the layers of stiff paper wrapping, and took the piece in her hands.

"So this is it," she whispered, and sat gazing at it for a while. I wasn't sure if she was happy or upset—or maybe a little of both.

{ { {

To tell the truth, I knew exactly how she felt, because I had once felt the same way. When I was first introduced to Akira through a friend of a friend, he was still in college. The moment our eyes met, I sensed something deeply spiritual about him, about every aspect of him: the light in his eyes, his small body, the way he moved. Something emanated from his being that seemed very familiar to me. I felt instantly repelled by him, but then, just as forcefully, irresistibly drawn to him.

In the village, I had studied some psychology, so I realized that someday my past would catch up with me. I would never escape unscarred. Although I couldn't anticipate what form the aftereffect would take, I knew that all I could do was to accept its inevitability as something that would come naturally.

Actually, I found it somewhat comforting that the word "aftereffect" sounded very much like "afterglow." My delayed reaction to my childhood caused me pain, but at least I felt relieved that it took the form of falling in love with a man like Akira, rather than suddenly having a nervous breakdown or something. I've heard of women who slide right into marriage with a nice guy at work, and everything seems happy until the bride decides she wants to strangle her own baby. Compared to that, I thought that I was handling things fairly reasonably.

I knew fully the weight of my earlier years, so I was resigned to the fact that there was bound to be some fallout, which made me very sad. As with people who have a family history of cancer or anemia, I felt burdened by the blood flowing in my veins, my inevitable destiny. I was who I was and could never become the child of any other mother and father.

When Akira and I first moved in together, I was in a very delicate emotional state, so he decided to make something for me. That turned out to be the first of the many amulets he created.

I wish you could have a chance to hold one in your hands, too. He made that one just for me, and there was nothing else like it in the world. I have no doubt, though, that anyone would find the shape appealing. Perhaps it's a similar sensation to when a baby suckles at her mother's breast and feels the nipple in her mouth for the very first time. That gentle shove toward the realization that someone accepts you totally and unconditionally. Akira's pieces have the power to communicate that.

The first time I held the amulet in the palm of my hand, I could feel a squall of warm tears pass through the sky of my heart. It felt so nice and sweet that it made my hand tingle. It reminded me of a time long ago, when I was a little girl, and someone had given me a newly hatched baby bird to hold.

Tears in my eyes, I said to Akira, "It's so beautiful, but I don't think I should keep it. I'm afraid I might break it or something and then what would I do?"

"If you lose this one, I can always make you another. I'd do that for you," he replied.

And, with those words, I felt as if I had woken from an extremely long dream, just like that. I realized it was what I'd been seeking all along. Of course I didn't know if it really signified anything, but to me it was the most important charm. And I needed something like that, after what I'd been through. I'd left my home and family and identity behind and was all by myself, and—though I didn't realize it—terribly lonely. And I was scared because I knew for a fact how you can have the earth beneath your feet yanked out from under you, and lose everything, all at once. Nothing seemed stable in my heart.

I wondered if the leader of the village had said something similar to my father. For the first time, I felt as though I had some understanding of what my father had experienced. When you're that moved by someone else's words, part of it has to be good timing, because what Akira said to me, or the leader to my father, might well have sounded trite or hackneyed to somebody else. It just rolls off the other person's tongue, as if it had no great significance, but I imagine that they realize somewhere deep, deep inside the power of what they've just said. You can feel that they've brought those words from some distant beautiful place just to give away to you.

{ { {

The customer said, "It's the strangest feeling, don't you think?"

"Really?" I replied.

"I heard about these amulets from a friend of mine," she said and looked straight into my eyes.

"I see."

I tried not to get too involved with the customers and their personal circumstances, but I could tell that I could trust this woman, and that she wouldn't go into great detail about her troubles, anyway. I let her tell her story.

"You see, I had several abortions when I was younger, but now that I actually have a husband, I can't get pregnant. I don't know if I should be telling you this, but—well, anyway, my husband's such a sweet guy, but I can't talk with him about it. My doctor examined me and said that there's no problem on my side."

"And then your friend told you about the amulets?"

"That's right. But then she said that he won't make them for just anyone, so I was a little worried," she said with a nervous laugh.

"I'm sure there's no problem," I reassured her.

Even though commissions for his work barely dribbled in, Akira had indeed turned down a few orders before. Somehow I could tell that he would have no objection to a person like the woman who sat before me. He didn't compare each potential customer to ones he'd worked for before, but rather seemed to be able to sense whether they were on the level or not.

Akira wanted to hear about their personal circumstances even less than I did. He told me that if he found out what a client was going through, he'd end up dwelling on that instead of concentrating on the piece itself.

And then there was the time a customer came and told Akira that his mother, who was in the hospital with terminal cancer, wanted one of Akira's amulets more than anything in the world. Akira told the man that he was not able to make one for her, and he refused to change his mind no matter how the man pleaded with him. He didn't give a particular reason. The man then started reminiscing about his mother and telling us what a wonderful woman she was, and about all the things she'd done for him. Despite this touching story, Akira would not take the order and, sensitive guy that he is, started crying. He told the man, "I don't think my amulet would be appropriate for your mother." Finally, the man went away, and I was left to comfort Akira, who sat weeping, confused about why he felt that he couldn't take that order.

The next day, we found out from someone that the man was a spy for a company that made religious objects. My reaction to that news was total shock: "I can't believe it! How pathetic that he would come to steal secrets from you. I thought he looked kind of seedy. You may be in the same business as him, but you're a million times better, Akira."

And Akira's reaction: "So, that's why I couldn't do it. Now it all makes sense to me." Period. This impressed me no end, and I understood why the two of us were together.

{ { {

The woman thanked me, put an envelope containing money on the table, and got up to leave. I felt certain that she had a chance at getting pregnant soon. We had just met, but I felt a great liking for her so I stood up and shook her hand firmly.

"Good luck. I hope that it works out for you," I told her.

Akira often gets mad at me because he thinks I'm too nice to strangers, and cold as a fish at home. What can I do? He's right, but that's the way I am. I'm more enthusiastic about people I've just met, whom I barely know at all, than with old friends. Before the awkwardness of a new acquaintance has worn off, I'm ready to offer myself up to that person.

{ { {

When I got back to the apartment, Akira was watching a video. It turned out to be the movie *The Right Stuff*. It was just at the scene where the astronauts are about to take off. They were all being pushed backwards by the force of gravity. I could tell from the expression on his face that Akira was right there with the astronauts, feeling their pain. When he was at home, Akira was just an ordinary guy, even a little wimpy, in fact. Sometimes when I saw him like that, I wondered where inside that small body lay the strength to create such amazing objects, objects that had the power to heal.

"Hi. Oh, a letter came for you," he said, pointing to the desk. "It's from your dad."

"From my father?" I said, surprised. I walked over to the desk and saw a thick envelope with my name on it, lying amidst the jumble of metalworking tools and other stuff.

{ { {

One month earlier, I'd seen my father for the first time in three years. I met him in Ueno Park, and I had

Akira come with me. The cherry blossoms had already scattered.

In March, Dad called me at work to tell me that he was coming to Tokyo to visit an old friend (not the man who had betrayed him, of course). He wanted to see me. I hadn't been expecting anything like that, because I didn't think Father would ever set foot in Tokyo again. I knew that he and my mother had not left the village for more than ten years. But even though he had been stuck there, for all that time, unable and unwilling to venture out, maybe now he was getting stronger, just maybe. That was my guess at first but then I realized that he was coming to Tokyo because he wanted to see me. To see me. The sect itself had no rigid rules about the followers' behavior, but I knew that for the leader to encourage my father to take such a long journey there had to be some very sound reason, like visiting his daughter.

I guessed—no, I felt certain—that my father would ask me to return to the village with him. Most likely, his methods of persuasion would get me right in the gut. If it had been in the days before I knew Akira, I definitely would not have agreed to see him. I had not yet become my own person, even though I'd been living apart from them. I would have been depressed and in tears his entire visit.

Just because you get married or live on your own doesn't mean that you're independent from your parents. Not at all. I've seen many people, not only living apart from their parents but also married and with children of their own, who are still carrying around their parents' legacy. I'm not criticizing them, just saying that they've never really grown up.

I found that out after I met Akira. And no, that's not because he and I joined together to create a wonderful new family or something soupy like that. It was because only after I met Akira did I truly understand what they mean when they say that all you really have is yourself. That's a terribly lonely realization. Despite my mother and my father and the village, despite the apartment I share with Akira, I am the only one in the world who knows what's best for me. I'm just here, deciding things I need to decide for myself.

It's difficult for me to explain.

I am my own home, and this is where I belong, and things keep going forward, endlessly, just as the blue of the sky before the dawn soon turns into a bright sunrise, each with its own beauty. That kind of thing.

If I had understood that sooner, I probably would never have left the village. I wouldn't have needed to. But I only made this realization after coming to Tokyo and after Akira and I met. I concluded quietly to myself that it's best to stay put.

We met Father on Sunday, April 10, in front of the Benten Shrine by Shinobazu Pond in Ueno. We chose that as a meeting place because Mom and Dad and I used to go there a lot to pray when we lived in Tokyo.

From the moment I woke up that morning, I was in a strange mood, because I dreaded seeing Dad again. I went back to bed and snuggled up with Akira, who was still trying to sleep and shooed me away. I dropped a bowl and broke it, which upset me so much that I burst into tears. Then I decided to sit down and read a comic, which made me laugh hysterically. I was a total mess. I didn't know what I was doing.

Originally, I had intended to go to the park by myself, but as the morning wore on, I could feel my chest tightening painfully. I decided that I would be okay if Akira was there with me and so I asked him if he would come along. Now, this is a man who usually resists going out to see people, but he said that he'd go with me. We were holding hands as we left the apartment.

It was springtime, and Shinobazu Pond looked peaceful, with many boats skimming across its calm surface. The sky, filled with dark, leaden clouds, seemed to be pressing down on us. Even though we arrived twenty minutes early, my father was already waiting in front of Benten Shrine. Just standing there, the same as he'd always been.

The moment I saw his figure, I stopped, not able to go any closer, and looked for a place to hide. I stood there and watched him. Akira didn't try to push me forward, but kept holding my hand, as relaxed as ever. I took in every detail: Father's gray jacket, his worn black shoes, his bald head, his erect posture. It made me want to scream.

Then all of a sudden it began to rain. Big drops came splashing down on us. I imagined that all the people in the rowboats on the pond were hurrying back to shore, but I couldn't see the pond from where we stood. Father didn't open his umbrella, but instead stood there, waiting for me. The rich brown wood of the shrine rose up large and vivid behind him. The gaudy colors of the souvenir stands looked forlorn as the rain soaked them. I could see Father so clearly. In profile, the shape of his eyebrow looked just like mine, and his eyes searched in earnest for me.

At that moment, Akira said, almost as if singing, "Your father's going to get soaked, Chikako. Are you going to just leave him out there with the shrine and the crows?"

He was right, of course. I moved toward my father.

"Dad. We're here."

I didn't cry. He smiled broadly, his eyes narrowing. I introduced Akira, who announced that he had to go home, but we wouldn't let him. We all went to a restaurant and had lunch together. Dad gave us some strawberry jam that Mom had made.

He never did tell me to come home. I started to

think that perhaps someday in the distant future, I would be able to go visit them in the village. Up until that moment, I hadn't even been able to conceive of such a thing because it scared me too much. Even though I hadn't actually decided to go, at least I could think of it as a possibility. It felt like it might work out okay. Like a student who goes to the big city for college, maybe someday I'd return to my home in the country.

> Dear Chikako,
>
> I was glad to see you in Tokyo, and I felt relieved to know that you've found yourself a nice young man. Your mother is happy for you too. Please thank Akira for the lunch. I enjoyed the grilled eel a great deal.
>
> I did not mention this to you during our visit but I had a difficult trip to Tokyo. The plane left behind schedule, and then it proved to be a very rough flight. While we were waiting to take off, I had an opportunity to talk with a number of other passengers and make their

acquaintance. It had been ages since I'd spoken with people outside the village, and it was actually very pleasant. I felt quite comfortable being with them. I met a young lady on her way to visit relatives in Tokyo, and a businessman who showed me the souvenirs he was taking home to his wife and children. There was also an elderly couple, and a young man traveling by himself.

Once we were in the air, we ran into what I assumed was turbulence, and the plane suddenly started bouncing roughly. This was unsettling enough, but then when we saw the frightened expression on the flight attendant's face as she tried to make her way down the aisle, everyone became extremely anxious. It was awful. In the end, of course, we arrived safely in Tokyo, but for a while I wondered whether we would. The way the plane was shaking was unbelievable. I could smell death in the cabin of that plane. I suppose that was because everyone on the flight at that moment thought that we were going to die.

I started chanting a sutra, and did not fear
death. I was very sad to see that the people
around me, who only moments before had had
smiles on their faces, now looked extremely
frightened. Some of them even vomited because
they were so scared. It hurt me so to think that
they were facing death without feeling at peace
with themselves. I suddenly felt as close to them
as I do to your mother, and our friends, and you,
and I pledged that I would remember them
smiling, rather than as I saw them then. I was
overcome with sorrow. It was also the first time
that I felt true affirmation for my faith in my
heart and soul.

When I was younger and without my belief,
I never would have noticed things like that. The
universe is the mind of the Buddha.

Your mother and I will continue our life
here in the village. You live your life to the
fullest there in Tokyo. No matter where you are,
you are loved and forgiven, and not only by us.

Take good care of yourself.

Dad

It was just what I had expected, and more. But, to tell the truth, his expression of faith had moved me.

"What a pious letter!" I said, annoyed.

"But a good one, huh?" Akira said, his eyes still on the TV screen.

"How do you know? Did you read it?" I asked.

"No, but I could tell from the expression on your face when you were reading it," he replied.

He and I fit together so well, like the swirl on the yin/yang symbol—his tough resilience and my resilient toughness.

Even if, for some reason, he couldn't make his amulets anymore, we'd get by. I'm not afraid of our money running out. I could always work in a bar or something. The only thing that scares me is time passing, like when the soft branches of a willow tree are warmed by the sunlight one moment and then ripped by a typhoon the next. As when the cherry blossoms bloom, only to fall to the ground. That this moment will end, with the warm orange sunlight streaming in onto Akira, as he lies curled up, watching his video, and night will come. That is the saddest thing to me.

"Let's go have soba at Chojuan," Akira said.

"Sounds great," I agreed. I would go out with Akira and forget, for a brief while, the sorrow that clings to life. I would pretend for a moment that my sadness might someday disappear.

A STRANGE TALE FROM

DOWN BY THE RIVER

When, exactly, did my sex life get so wild? I honestly can't remember. I do know that I tried absolutely everything. I did it with women; I did it with men. I did it in groups. I tried it outdoors. I tried it in foreign countries. The only things I steered clear of were tying people up and getting tied up, getting high on drugs, and necrophilia. That kind of stuff gave me the creeps.

In the end, I realized that sex isn't that different from any other pastime. You have your people who are rank amateurs at sex, and others who are masters of the art. Some people think of nothing else, while others merely dabble in it. A few approach eroticism with the loftiest of motives, while others might as well be rolling around in the gutter, they're so base. Like people who are fond of sitting at a pottery wheel and making ceramics all day, or baking bread, or playing the violin, you can get hooked on sex and never, ever let go. Of course, I'm not saying that devoting yourself to sex is comparable to more noble ways of occupying yourself, only that some people get involved with sex the same way they might with any other hobby, high or low.

Everyone has her own *michi*, or path in life. People live to find their own *michi*. That's certainly what I'd been searching for. I thought that I could use sex as a means of forging my own way. I enjoyed doing it in different settings with different people and experiencing so many different emotions. That's what it all meant to me: the delicious sensations of pleasure that I shared with them, those hours of ecstasy when I felt my body melt into my soul. The clear blue sky threatening to expose me, sunlight, glistening green leaves. The daytime hours, which only reminded me of how much I had to hide from the night before.

But my intention here is not just to write about sex, because, in the end, I think I got into it as a matter of chance, because I had lots of energy, and not because I was particularly cut out for sex. It could have just as easily been something else—ceramics, cooking, or music. I will admit that I craved the feeling of liberation, the release, and loved the anticipation and excitement when we experimented with entirely new ways of making love, and the intensity of desire that drives you to the edge. Sex turned on a switch that made me feel the mind-body connection.

It was when I came down with a liver infection that I had to quit going to the sex parties. That's the real reason I gave it up.

{ { {

After my health improved, my father helped me find a proper job as a secretary at a computer programming firm. Sometimes when I was talking with my new friends at work, I'd wonder if perhaps I did have some special talent for sex after all. I used to be so totally involved in sex that it never even occurred to me that I might be different. But I had done it so many times that I guess I could be considered an expert. None of the other girls my age seemed to have much sexual experience, and the way they talked about it struck me as childish and naive. My past had equipped me with a certain degree of confidence.

And then I met my boyfriend. We'd known each other for a month before we first went out (that was about a year ago). From the first date, we got along real well.

He worked at one of the firms that my company did business with. He had one brother, who was quite a bit older. Their father had passed away in July, and my boyfriend's brother had taken over the family's business.

In fact, we met at his father's funeral, which I attended in my boss's place. The ritual moved me tremendously. People had told me what a dignified, splendid man the president had been, how he had run his business innovatively and with integrity. I had also heard that his employees loved working for him. When I saw the many people who came to pay their last respects, I knew all these stories must be true.

The funeral came as a revelation to me. Everyone willingly set aside quarrels from the past and came together to lament his passing and express their grief. Utterly sincere in their sadness, all of the mourners prayed for the repose of the deceased. The whole thing was almost too beautiful, the birth, life, and death of the man portrayed as totally sublime. For those few hours, the deceased and everyone who knew him were forgiven and forgave.

The floral wreaths looked elegant, and all of the offerings suggested great care and sensitivity. The priests chanted the sutras with dignity and solemnity, and I could sense a feeling of unity among all the mourners, who were glad for the opportunity to commemorate his life. The only times that I had ever experienced such a circle of energy in a gathering of people—although it may seem irreverent to compare the two occasions—were the orgies with my favorite friends.

At the funeral, the man who was to become my boyfriend escorted his mother, who, despite her advanced years, was as distraught as a young widow might have been. Everything about her black garments and her manner bespoke the depth of her grief. I could sense the beauty, if that is the correct term, of their love for each other, as well as her resignation in the face of her husband's death.

He stayed at his mother's side constantly, like a shadow, and the black of their funeral kimonos seemed veiled in their grief and powerful determination to make it through the day. I couldn't keep my eyes off them, and continued to watch, through every stage of the ceremony, from the lighting of the incense to the removal of the coffin from their home. A bewitching field of energy seemed to surround the pair, energy that took the form of a group of people who had joined together to speak praise of their late husband and father's life.

I was not being subtle about my attraction, and he noticed me early in the day. Each time our eyes met, I wanted so badly to say something to him, to comfort him.

I knew that he was barely older than me, but he carried himself with such maturity and dignity throughout what must have been one of the most trying days of his life. I wondered if I could have done the same. I could sense how alone, both spiritually and socially, he was feeling, despite the crowd of friends and relatives right there with him. I also felt that only I could truly understand his emotions that day, and also, in some sense, that I already knew him and loved him.

I didn't want to leave, but finally I went over and bowed stiffly to the family before departing. I really, truly wanted to see him again, and felt certain that I would.

And, of course, I did. Not too long after the funeral, he called and asked me out.

{ { {

He proposed sometime later, during dinner at his place.

"I was wondering—would you consider marrying me?"

"Yes, of course," I replied, just like that.

His apartment was on the second floor of a building that overlooked the river, so close that when the windows were open you could hear the water flowing. If you stood by the window on a windy day, you could even smell the muddiness of the river below, and, at the same time, see the glittering lights of the city reflected in the water, and the moon lingering in the sky above.

At the beginning, I walked along the riverbank every day, headed toward his apartment, as if I would never return. We only saw each other once a week, but sometimes I would stay the night at his place. Before long, I found myself going directly from his place to my office in the morning.

I always listened to the voice of the river, saying to me, "I flow along endlessly. I am constant." Those murmurs engulfed me, like a lullaby, which soothed me and my anxiety about our love.

I actually felt somewhat uneasy about the fact that he lived in such a large, fancy apartment. After all, he was still in his twenties. It wasn't as if I were unused to comfort: my father was also a company president, small though his business was, and I had gone to a private girls' school where success was guaranteed. You could call me a princess, I guess. All the same, I felt somewhat taken aback by his uncompromising love for "true beauty" and his ability to own such *objets*.

After he'd moved in, he had taken care to select every single piece of furniture and fine china in the apartment according to his own taste, such as it was. It seemed so overdone to me that, if it hadn't been that particular apartment by the river, I might have been intimidated by his fastidiousness and fled. But he wasn't weird or anything. I came to understand that it was the view from his window that had attracted him to the apartment in the first place—those big windows, and the river. The river was the core, the center of the apartment.

The window framed a fantastic, dynamic scene outside, like a living picture. Boats chugged by; the streetlights and buildings lit up as dusk crept over the city. The river made music to fill those rooms.

He had been able to capture the powers of nature so evident in the river, and bring them into his home, as one does with bonsai. It was fascinating to me how he had conceived of the vitality of nature and its competing forces as interior design. He had had nothing to do with making the scene outside his home, of course, but rather his possessions and the location of his home, on the riverbanks, complemented each other. Creating a harmonious space seemed to have been his plan, and an indication of his spirit. Everything in the apartment was him.

I wanted to live in this apartment, because I sought to become part of him, and his home, and part of the timeless space there. As I stood by the open window, and felt the chill of the wind blowing off the broad river, I longed to blend into that scene.

{ { {

"I knew you'd say yes," he said. "But, I've got to tell you, I'm kind of concerned that whoever gives the toast at the reception might stand up and say, 'It was love at first sight when they met at his father's funeral.' It sounds like an inauspicious beginning, don't you think?"

"You're right, it does. But people don't always have to spell things out exactly as they happened. I've heard all sorts of lies at my friends' weddings."

"I guess I'll have to take your word for it. If it's okay with you, then, I'll go and have a talk with your parents soon. I have to ask for your hand, don't I? Maybe I'll go right away."

I felt overjoyed to see him so happy.

"Why don't I call them and tell them? They'll be so excited for us. I know they will. I think you'll like them," I said, smiling. "Plus, they already know that I have a boyfriend, and they probably assume that there's something serious going on anyway, considering my age and all. Don't worry."

If there was something to worry about, it was that an important piece was missing from my life. Even though I would literally throw myself into things, I was eternally skimming the surface, never truly hearing or seeing the substance. All along, I'd look for surface beauty to hide the emptiness. But perhaps that's what hobbies are for, in the final analysis.

I think there was also a big hole in my boyfriend's existence as well, although perhaps for a different reason. That's probably why there was a place for me in his home. Although there are many married couples like that, I found it unsettling that it was so patently obvious to me.

I knew that I was at home there, because the river flowed by outside the windows.

Somehow, I could never feel at ease. I felt so blue all of the time, always distracted and thinking about someplace else, far away. And I constantly had the sound of the river on my mind, whether I was eating lunch, or changing my clothes, or sleeping, or drinking coffee in a bright room flooded with morning sunlight.

I felt as if I had forgotten something important, that there was something I should regret.

Those parts of me merged with the apartment and the view from the windows, and took on a life of their own. The ones that accepted me, him, and the windows and the river.

{ { {

"But it's such a famous, wealthy family. How are you going to fit in?" my mother asked.

I hadn't been home for quite a while. As I expected, my father didn't raise any objections to the marriage. My older sister and brother were both already married, so he was used to it. In fact, he hardly seemed to notice what I told him, and went out to play mahjongg with friends, leaving Mom and me alone in the living room. My older brother and his wife had gone to a party somewhere, and weren't home either.

My parents had a lovely home in an upper middle class neighborhood, like something out of a magazine. Everyone lived the same kind of life there. Only I didn't quite fit in, even though I was from the same mold.

Mom went out to the kitchen and returned with a bottle of wine and two glasses. She'd been saving the wine for a special occasion like this, she told me. After I'd had some wine and was feeling fairly relaxed, I confessed my conflicting feelings.

"It'll be fine, though, I'm sure. He doesn't have any big family responsibilities. He can spend his time any way he pleases."

"I've always had the feeling that's what you'd like, and it turns out to be true, doesn't it?" Mother said.

"What do you mean?"

"That you've always seemed a little out of touch with reality. You're such a dreamer, Akemi! But I have to admit that of all the kids you were always the best about helping around the house and taking out the garbage. You never even complained about having to walk the dog. I don't know—on the one hand, I feel like I need to shake you and tell you about the realities of marriage. It's not just some pretty dream, you know. But maybe you'll do okay. Plus—I know this may sound a bit crass—but it makes a big difference if you don't have to worry about money."

It was exactly what I had expected her to say, and I loved her for it.

My father didn't fool around with other women, but he did spend most of his time apart from my mother, with his ceramics collection. He had gone through all sorts of money buying pots, sometimes at outlandish prices. According to Mom, if Dad hadn't had his ceramics, he certainly would have had lots of girlfriends instead. She was no fool. That's why she let him putter around with his pots and tea bowls.

My mother didn't mince words, and I imagine she was right about Dad. Compared to my boyfriend's father, my dad was not cut out to be in charge of a company. He was too sensitive and kind for that, but he still had to make big decisions and decide how much his employees would make, so he needed his hobby to keep himself sane.

Hobby. Somehow this seems to be a key concept, in my childhood, and in my whole life.

"I think you have your head screwed on right, but you also seem unsettled, as if you could fly away any minute. Maybe that's because you were born by the river," Mom said.

"What? What do you mean?"

"Just what I said. You were born by the river."

"That can't be. I always thought you had me in a hospital in Tokyo," I objected. I knew that my brother and sister had been born in the same hospital.

"No, I never told you about that?" Mom said. "I had you in a small clinic in the town where I grew up. Your father was having problems with his business at the time, and he and I weren't getting along well either. I was very depressed, so I went back to my parents' home to have you. Their house was right by the river, and you could see the water and the dike from my room.

"I threw myself into taking care of our home and you kids when Dad was away so much. I just wore myself out. By the time you were born, the most I could manage was to sit and hold you and watch the river go by. I think we spent about six months there, until Dad came to take us home. I was so lonesome."

Surprised, I said to her, "I had no idea, Mom. . . . Did you ever think of jumping into the river and taking me with you?"

"Absolutely not," she answered, laughing to herself. Then she looked at me and smiled, without a trace of ambivalence.

"No, I was never that desperate. I spent most of my time thinking, because I didn't have enough energy to do anything else. I've never been so calm in my life, before or since, as I was then. You know, I'd just sit there, trying to remember the name of the red flowers on that tree over there, or wondering what the old man who came down for a walk by the river each day was thinking about when he stood there, staring into the water. Everything about the place was so familiar to me since I'd grown up there, and it reminded me so much of my childhood days. I suppose that I needed that time at home. It wasn't so bad."

There's something she's not telling me, I thought. She was presenting her memories of those days so elegantly, and portraying herself in such a positive light. I stared at my wineglass, unable to listen any longer.

{ { {

Some time later, after we'd become engaged, I received an interesting phone call at work. It was a winter evening, around five o'clock.

"Is that you, Akemi?" It was a woman's voice, but,

for the life of me, I couldn't tell who it might be. "I understand that you're going to get married."

Finally I recognized the voice. It was a friend from my old life, a well-to-do married woman.

"That's right, I am," I replied.

"I just happened to run into K, and he told me. Do you still see people from the old group?"

"No, I got sick and gave that all up," I said with a laugh.

"Well, your body is your most valuable possession, after all!" I could hear her laugh on the other end of the line.

I'm the type who doesn't keep up with old friends. Like when I entered middle school, I stopped playing with my pals from grade school. It's too much of a bother to do so many things at once.

And in the case of those particular adult friends, we would hardly even say hello to one another in public because it was too embarrassing to acknowledge them in the light of day. That's why, once I stopped going to the parties, my relationships with them ended. Significantly, I barely even missed them at all.

I felt somewhat differently about this particular

woman, though. If anyone else from those days had phoned, I probably would have hung up on them, or just listened, and not very politely at that. I was glad to hear from her, though, and happy that she had remembered me.

She was, of course, one of our group. She was staying at a cottage in Karuizawa one summer, and put out the word that she was looking for a companion, a sensitive, caring woman who didn't need babysitting. I hadn't met her before but decided to join her anyway. I stayed with her in Karuizawa for a week, and then we left for a two-week trip to Hokkaido, leaving behind her husband, who was occupied with a mistress, anyway. I hadn't seen her since, and it had been five years since I'd spoken with her.

"I just wanted to congratulate you."

"Thanks so much."

"Once you're married, you can't be active the way you used to be. You know that, don't you? There's something so special about you. I hope you don't mind me saying that."

"What do you mean, something special?" I asked.

"When I was with you, I just knew that I was safe.

And it always seemed so fresh, like something new was going to happen at every moment. How can I describe it? I don't know—a feeling of anticipation, maybe? New possibilities?

"Remember our trip to Hokkaido? I really didn't feel like going, but I had a great time anyway. You have the ability to create your own little world—Akemi's world—and that will never change. And I enjoyed just watching you, like watching a movie. I felt comfortable with you, and I didn't have to do anything, just sit there. I felt drawn to you. I didn't want to let you go. I really wanted to hold on."

She spoke slowly, choosing each word carefully.

"So even I couldn't make you happy," I said.

"Happy? I don't think of life in those terms. I had a good time traveling with you, I really did. Is there anything better than that? It's a blessing to have a spark in your soul, something wild," she continued. "But you can't behave like that forever. You're not a child anymore, and it's not becoming in an adult. Plus, you've got to be careful about AIDS. You have to know when to quit."

"I'm glad you called."

"I wish you all the happiness in the world," she said. That was it. We both knew that she'd never call again.

{ { {

I still had vivid memories of our days together. The first time we met, she looked me over with the utmost care, not critically, but as if she were appraising me. She had greeted me at the door in her bathrobe. I had on a black leather jacket and jeans. I didn't know exactly how long I'd stay, so I had packed a big overnight bag. In fact, it was my favorite Louis Vuitton satchel, made of green snakeskin. I still use that bag, but at the time I had just bought it and was excited at having a chance to show it off.

I had much more fun than I expected. We ended up being a pretty odd couple. It was kind of touching. She liked to cook, but she couldn't just whip up meals. Instead, she'd spend hours making plates of fancy little finger foods. Like many wealthy women, she wasn't so much interested in having sex with other women as in savoring the companionship and the general mood of the hours we spent together. But I liked her because she was very smart and pretty, too.

After she invited me in, she made a clumsy attempt to make a fire in the fireplace. I went over and offered to help her. By the time we finally got the logs burning, our hands and faces were black with soot. We bathed in a sweet little marble tub with lion claw feet.

Later she poured two glasses of whiskey, and we curled up by the fireplace with our drinks, quietly waiting for night to come. I enjoyed sitting there with her, waiting for what we both knew would eventually happen between us. I didn't feel as if we were just lusting after each other, but rather that we both anticipated a certain splendor, as one does when one looks forward to watching a sunset after a fine day. It was obvious to me that she was feeling a lot of pain, and needed an escape.

At last, we pulled the antique lace spread off the bed and lay down together. I realized that she had probably made love with her husband in that very bed. Our own lovemaking was graceful and lasted for hours, in perfect harmony with our elegant surroundings.

The next morning when I woke up, I felt as

though she and I had been together in the mountain cottage for many years. The rays of sun filtering in through the woods seemed to pierce my heart and fill me with longing. I loved her sweet smell and the soft, round curves of her body.

During the days that followed, we spent the afternoons watching movies on the VCR and waiting for the long, warm nights. We didn't have much to talk about and hardly ever laughed, but I had a good time anyway. We were high up in the mountains, where the air was so thin that I thought I'd melt into the brilliant blue sky above the treetops. When she invited me to go to Hokkaido with her, I felt curious about how long we could keep it up, and what would happen between us. But nothing changed. She would reach out for me repeatedly, and I made love to her gently, bringing her to the point of ecstasy again and again.

One day, at the hotel in Hokkaido, a phone call came from her husband. After they had argued for a while, she put her foot down and told him that she would divorce him if he didn't come back to live with her. That ended our brief romance. I felt forlorn, because we had done so many fun things together. We'd watched lots of movies and gone shopping in the market. We'd spent hours on the ski slopes, and then gone back to the lodge to drink mugs of hot coffee and complain about our sore legs.

But I always sensed that eventually it would end. Our time in the country together had been so perfect that I knew it wouldn't work if we tried it again in Tokyo. Sometimes that's what happens with relationships that are too perfect. The only thing to do is to end them.

On the plane back to Tokyo, I was so distraught that I could barely speak. I wanted to cry. She was wearing sunglasses, but I could tell that she was pretty upset, too. We parted at Haneda Airport in Tokyo. As we were saying good-bye, she gave me a thick envelope with a pretty floral design on it.

I watched her disappear into the crowd of people at the taxi stand and realized that I'd never see her again. It seemed strange to be without her, after spending all those days together, holding hands and kissing. I even knew the softness inside her panties. I was going to miss her.

Inside the envelope, I found 500,000 yen in cash,

and two photos she'd taken with a Polaroid. One was of me standing in the woods at Karuizawa, drenched in sunlight and waving at the camera, the blue sky my backdrop. In the other, I was lying naked in bed, drinking lemonade and reading a magazine. I didn't know exactly why she'd given them to me. Perhaps she wanted to forget everything or didn't want to leave any evidence of our time together. Maybe she was just being sentimental. In any case, the pictures made me think longingly of our lost days together, and I decided to keep them. In fact, I still have them.

{ { {

About a week after I heard from her at work, I was hanging out in a cafe in Aoyama, sipping a large cup of espresso. And who walked in but K. It was my fate, I knew, for me to run into him again. Something new was happening. My wedding wasn't far off, and I recognized that my past was not going to disappear so easily.

By then, I had resigned from my company and had no real reason to be in that part of town. In fact, I could easily have gone over to my fiancé's place and used his espresso machine, if I'd wanted to drink some. But I sometimes got a craving for the weak coffee they served at the cafe in Aoyama.

That day, I had stopped on my way home from shopping. It was about six o'clock in the evening. I was sitting there, totally relaxed and daydreaming, so I didn't even notice that this man, whom I would normally have gone out of my way to avoid, was heading in my direction. Frankly, though, if there was anyone whom I thought I should see one more time before I got married, it was K. I felt as if I had somehow unconsciously summoned him.

"Akemi," he addressed me by name. When I looked up and saw the powerful light in his eyes, I suddenly had the urge to pretend that I didn't know him. But I didn't think fast enough and lost my chance to stare at him blankly and then just turn away.

"It's been years," I said to him, trying my best to look annoyed.

He didn't flinch, but smiled and went to get a cup of coffee. He came back and sat across from me.

"So you're getting married, I hear," he said.

"And you've been spreading the word, I hear."

"I just couldn't believe my ears, so I had to tell someone. I didn't mean any harm."

"What are you up to these days, now that the bubble has burst?"

In the old days, K had his own business importing accessories and antiques from Spain or someplace. He was extremely aggressive and was always asking high prices, but people liked him anyway because he seemed so sophisticated. But I'd heard that the business had since failed.

"Now? Same kind of stuff. I came up with the idea of a late-night French food delivery service, and it's been very profitable. I have no trouble at all finding young guys to work for me, what with everyone so underemployed these days. At the start, I was really into it, and would spend a lot of time reading up on different cooking techniques. These days, though, I'm more into keeping the business going."

"You've been through a lot."

"I like my life now."

"How's everybody doing?"

"Getting along well, and no one is HIV-positive."

"Glad to hear it."

"I hope you don't mind me saying this," he said, "but once you get involved in playing like that, you can never get out of it totally. Especially someone like you. You're the kind who gets all excited at work, just thinking of the weekend, I bet."

"Actually, I seem to have forgotten all about it. Being in the hospital made me forget," I said.

"It doesn't surprise me to hear you say that. You always seemed above it all. I always thought it was just cheap narcissism, but maybe you were looking for something different from the rest of us."

"I'm only interested in what I'm involved in at the moment."

"So are you really excited about being a married lady? Does that powerful family make you feel secure? Will you be satisfied with a fancy house and a comfortable life?"

He was just being honest, not mean. I recalled that he had behaved the same way in bed. Then, all of a sudden, it came rushing back, the mood, the emotional intensity of those days. I felt overwhelmed for one brief moment.

"I just can't go back. Just like I couldn't go back to

kindergarten after first grade. I'm not interested in that kind of sex anymore."

"But you were so passionate, so strong. I've never met a woman who's so intense."

"Maybe so, but I've done my time, and I don't need it anymore. Believe me. Are you criticizing me for doing what I want to do and nothing else? I'm not the only one, either. Who are you to say what people should be doing with their emotions, anyway?" I challenged him.

I sensed something strange about him, a feeling I'd never had before. Maybe he'd gotten a little weird after exposing himself to so many people. Most people only show that much of their bodies to a spouse, or maybe a doctor.

"You had a talent for it, though, and I didn't."

"A talent for what? Sex?" I laughed.

"No, for living. You know all the right techniques, all the secrets. You understand how to flow with time, and not get stuck in one place. Once you master one thing and have done it enough, you move on. Or at least you're good at pretending to move on. I think most people live their whole lives repeating the same patterns, again and again and again."

"I'm not sure I get your point," I said. "I think I got sick of the group, of how exclusive it was, and how we'd just chew up new people and spit them out. For a while there, we were really cooking. I remember being fearless, to the point that I'd do anything. It couldn't get any better. I didn't care if it was day or night—I just wanted more.

"But then things started to break down, and it got to be a real bore. Have you ever ridden on the Space Mountain ride at Disneyland?"

"What does that have to do with anything?"

"Well, have you?"

"No."

"Once I did and it was so great. When you're flying through the Spiral of Death with all those people, you really get this feeling that you're at one with them. I was screaming all the way down, just like the foreigners, and it was such a trip to be right there in Chiba Prefecture, on that ride, on a beautiful summer day. It really got to me, experiencing the same thrill as a bunch of other people I'd probably never see again, and going so, so fast. But that type of intensity is only possible because the ride lasts only three minutes."

"Right."

"It seems like it was kind of the same with sex. Once that instant of pleasure was past, I always felt like I didn't want to be there anymore. Maybe I just overdid it."

The more I talked, the more fantastic my story became. I didn't care to share my real story with him, but instead told him what he wanted to hear. Not that I was lying to him, but I wasn't really talking about myself.

I had left the group, as a piece of ripe fruit falls from a tree and is swept away by the current of the river, and finally finds its proper place. So why did I bother giving him an explanation? Maybe because I had once respected him. Or maybe because I regretted having to give it all up.

K said, "Do you remember what you were like back then? You were wild. You really got me excited, but you scared me, too. Sometimes I thought you'd lost your mind, that you were so starved you'd gone over the edge. I've been with lots of people since then, but I've never seen anyone as earnest and crazy as you, baby. That's why it really amazed me when I heard that you were getting married. I wonder if you'll been able to forget that craving."

I thought, You just don't get it, do you? I didn't really put myself into it that much, and, in fact, I never even felt that tired afterward. I was just like a child, getting so involved in what I was doing that I forgot to eat and sleep. That's all. Maybe our capacities are totally different, or something. You are just the kind of person who would spend his entire life going to the group every single weekend, and I'm not.

But of course I couldn't say that to him.

K was enjoying his life in his own way, and he didn't care if that had drained him over the years, or warped his personality and the way he related to other people.

"You're the only one who could, baby." (That was the second time he had called me "baby.") "I didn't think you were the marrying kind. You used to like partying. He must really be something, your fiancé. Is he that rich?"

After I got sick and stopped going to the group, I felt rather strange. I had already found a job to distract me, but I was still going through a rough time psychologically. For about six months, I found that my cheeks would start twitching when I tried to talk, especially if I was tired or at a dinner party where I didn't especially want to be. I realized that indulging constantly in sex was potentially as harmful as stuffing your face with food all day. I paid for it in the end.

Eventually, though, I started feeling more normal, and only had sex once in a while, like most people. I went to work, ate lunch with people from the office, went clothes shopping. I got up in the morning and went to bed at night; my skin would break out and clear up. I stopped having those terrible attacks of lust that were symptoms of withdrawal from my addiction.

While I was learning to appreciate that there are other pleasures in life besides sex, K had kept doing what he'd always done, with members of our group, and their friends, in all kinds of places and all kinds of different positions. That realization freaked me out, and made me feel glad about my new life. I had done the right thing, seizing the opportunity to escape when I could. It even made me feel that there must be a God, who showed me the importance of good timing.

{ { {

"See you around," he said as he stood up to go.

"Yeah, see you," I replied, in the full realization that I would never see him again, unless, perhaps, I bumped into him at the cafe.

I paid my check and left. I walked slowly past the antique shops along the boulevard, and thought about K.

I was crazy about you, too. I really was.

The hem of my coat danced in the cold late-autumn wind. The shadows of the buildings stretched long down the street, so dark that it seemed the sun would never shine there again.

With your body, you embraced people and you pushed them away after you were done—so many times that it filled me with sorrow. But, to me, there was something special about you, something that no one else had. I could lose myself in that, and forget about time.

If you'd only been a bit gentler just now, and less jaded, if you hadn't assumed that vulgar familiarity when you talked with me, I might have let down my defenses, and gone to spend the night with you somewhere. We could have run away together, just the two of us, and hidden out for a month or maybe even more. We'd have found a cozy little flat where we could have made love, day and night. Forgetting everything, ruining my plans for marriage—even if it had meant that—I might have gone with you.

But you didn't realize that, and you looked to me like an abandoned newborn puppy, wrapped in a membrane of loneliness and humiliation. I can't connect with you anymore. We're in totally different realms.

I kept walking, mulling the encounter over and over in my mind. Then someone on a bicycle passed me. On the back, in a child seat, sat a little girl of about five. Oblivious to the speed at which her mother was pedaling along, the girl's eyes focused on me, the wind sweeping through her fine hair. She had a mature, almost adult face, and wore an expression of ennui, as if she were mourning something, as if she looked down on everything.

That's just how I am, I thought. As a metaphor for my life, it was completely on the mark. I had people to cart me around, protect me, spoil me. I lived peacefully in this country, Japan, living an unremarkable life, but feeling for all the world that I was special, and that I had seen and done so much more than everyone else I knew. I had pretended to drown myself in sex, but I actually hadn't even taken that many risks.

Even with that realization, I wasn't about to run off to Africa and dig wells for people who needed them, though I wished that I could. I would live and die, hopelessly ensconced in the cynical ways of the city.

I didn't even know what hope was. Even if something like that existed, shining and sparkling brightly somewhere, way beyond my reach, I knew that I couldn't absorb its force. Anyway, it wasn't in this town, nor could I find it in the eyes of the people I saw on the street. It didn't seem to exist on TV, or in any department store. That's how I grew up, listening to people at the next table talking about such trivial things that it made me want to puke.

K still thinks he can find it in sex. He lives as if that were the answer, as if that were hope. I grew weary of that way of living, and decided to make a bunch of altars and place myself on them. I don't know whether my way is better or not, but I'm comfortable with what I've chosen. In some ways, though, I also feel like I'm running around in circles. I feel certain that my confusion won't disappear even after I've had my gorgeous wedding and seen my parents' tears of joy. Or even after I've given birth to a child of my own and felt her weight in my own arms.

I don't know whether it's because of the times, or because of the kind of person I am, or because something that used to exist has disappeared. Once in a while, I get sucked into this maze, and everything seems distant, and all sensations, and joy, and pain vanish. In the end, my sorrow and my sense of beauty are only transformed into the landscape of a miniature garden. What an incomplete existence. I felt so, so down.

Perhaps the ghosts from the past had wielded their last burst of energy and were now dwelling in a dark channel.

{ { {

One Saturday, I was getting ready to go over to my boyfriend's apartment when the doorbell rang. I thought maybe it was someone delivering a package, but, to my surprise, I found my father standing there. I couldn't believe that he had come to visit me alone, without my mother.

"I'm on my way to work," he said. "I have a taxi waiting for me downstairs, so I can't stay long."

Though Dad had been slender and athletic as a young man, he'd put on a lot of weight in middle age. He lowered his bulk onto one of the chairs in my living room. In his hands, he carried a large package.

"What's that?" I asked.

"I wanted to give you something nice, so I went through the storage room and found this. It's a ceramic piece—Bizen ware. I hope that you'll use it, and not just leave it on a shelf somewhere."

He untied the wrapping cloth, and opened up the wooden box inside. It was a large, heavy piece.

"Thanks."

I smiled happily, knowing that Dad had come to give me a wedding present that meant something to him. I had assumed he would leave right away, because we didn't have any more to say to each other, but he remained seated.

"Is there something that you wanted to talk about?" I asked.

"Well, actually . . ." he said hesitantly. "I couldn't decide whether I should tell you this or not, but . . ."

"What?"

"Until quite recently, I really didn't see any reason for you to know, but when I realized that his apartment is down by the river, I thought we'd better have a talk."

"Does this have something to do with Mom?" I asked. Why else would he have come alone?

"Yes, it does. And the place where you were born."

"You always told me that I was born in the same hospital as the other kids, but that wasn't true, was it? That's what Mom said."

Sadly, Father replied, "When your mother was pregnant with you, things at the company weren't going so well. I also had a lover. When the company failed, I thought of leaving your mother and marrying the other woman, but then your mother was having emotional problems, and then you were born. With so many troubles in my life, my relationship with the other woman went sour."

"Did Mom know about her?" I asked.

"Of course she did. That's what made her get so depressed."

He still looked very sad. That day I learned yet one more reason why my father had put his family first and devoted himself to his pottery after I was born. I saw an entirely different course my life might have taken, because of that other life that he had been preparing for me. Or maybe he hadn't been thinking of me at all.

"Did she tell you that the two of you stayed in that house by the river for about six months after you were born? You were with your grandmother who lives in Tokyo now."

"Yes, she told me that."

"I came to see you for the first time when you were six months old. When I got to Grandma's house, your mother wasn't there, and when I asked about her, Grandma just smiled and said, 'She's down by the river.' She was smiling, but I sensed that she was trying to tell me something.

"I decided to go and find her. That river had such steep banks that you couldn't walk all the way to the water's edge, so if you wanted to get close and watch the current, you had to stand on the big bridge that crossed it. The bridge wasn't wide enough for cars, but it was sizable.

"When I got closer, I saw your mother leaning

over the railing, with you in her arms. It scared the hell out of me, and I'm sure if there had been anyone else around, they would have wanted to pull her back from there, too.

"She was holding you, but she was leaning way out, looking down at the water. I don't think that she was conscious of what she was doing. You were right over the water. I walked over to her and said hello, and she turned to me and smiled, just like she had when we met the very first time, on the first date arranged by our matchmaker. And she even let me hold her in my arms for a minute.

"We were standing there talking, when, all of a sudden, she became quiet. I asked her if everything was all right, but she became hysterical and started scream-ing. Then she threw you into the river. I jumped in and pulled you out. Luckily, the place you landed wasn't that deep, and there was hardly any current, so you weren't hurt. By the time I got you to the hospital, you were already smiling again.

"Your mom, though, was in a state of shock and barely conscious. Her whole body got rigid and she wouldn't respond to anyone. After an hour or so, she came out of it, and kept crying and apologizing to you. We had to put her in a hospital in Tokyo for a while after that.

"I did a lot of thinking and decided that I had done wrong by her. I wanted to make a fresh start. I went to see her in the hospital every day. By that time, your mother understood that she had been suffering from exhaustion and that she had needed professional help, and even the reasons for her breakdown, but I don't think she remembered about dropping you into the river. Even now, I think she has no memory of that. I'm just guessing though. Anyhow, in other ways, she recovered, so when she got out of the hospital, we started living together again as a family.

"Your brother might have realized that something strange was going on, but I don't think your sister was old enough to understand what was happening. So only Grandma and I really knew, and we kept it to ourselves.

"I even went to the doctor to ask if that incident might have damaged you psychologically. But you never seemed afraid of water when you were growing up, and I couldn't detect anything else. But now that you're getting married, I figured that I should tell you. Sometimes when people get married, old wounds from the past resurface."

I wasn't surprised at what he told me. On the contrary, I felt relieved, as if I had been able to confirm something I had known all along. The feeling of relief overwhelmed me so much that for a minute I couldn't speak.

"I hope that I haven't shocked you," he said.

"No. No, maybe if we were having problems, I might not have been able to handle it, but I'm okay," I reassured him. "And anyway, as long as I can remember, things have been good at home."

"That's true," Father replied, looking relieved. "You're like a guardian angel to me, Akemi. After you came into my life, I got my business back on track and I haven't had an affair since, either. I survived that dangerous period in my life."

I may have been wounded emotionally, I thought, but I can survive too. Perhaps that's what I gained from that secret incident with my mother, a self-confidence that I would always carry with me.

After Dad left, I took a taxi over to my boyfriend's. I took the ceramic bowl with me and told him that Father had given it to us. He loved beautiful things, and look very pleased with this new gift.

"We can use it together after we're married," he said happily.

And we talked about what we could serve in it—vegetable dishes, or pilaf would set it off nicely—and how we wanted to use it every day, and not just for special occasions. As we chattered away, I gradually forgot what Father had told me, and even the image of my mother's smiling face when she had insisted that she had never ever considered jumping into the river. That was what had shocked me—my mother's carefree expression. But all that faded away as I enjoyed my time with my fiancé in the bright room, talking and sipping a delicious cup of hot green tea.

That's all I wanted.

No one can survive childhood without being wounded. Everyone remembers at least one time when their parents rejected them, pushed them away, even though they may have still been in the womb, blind, and unable to speak. That's why, as adults, we all look for someone to become our parents again, and for someone to look after us in times of need. And we search for a person to live with who can provide the companionship we so desperately want.

My fiancé and I went out to a restaurant to have a bite to eat, and when we got back to his apartment, he decided to take a bath. I went into the kitchen for some reason or other, and I noticed a letter lying there on the counter. I don't know why it caught my eye, or even why I bothered looking at it. I never read his mail, and I could tell that it wasn't a woman's handwriting, so there was nothing in the least suspicious about it. Somehow, though, the way the letter was addressed attracted my attention, and impulsively I decided to take a look. I had never done anything like that in my life, but I felt completely at ease, not as if I were snooping. On the contrary, I felt compelled to open it.

But there was no letter inside. Instead, I found several photographs. When I saw what they were, I nearly fainted. They were compromising pictures of me. Some were in K's apartment, and others in a hotel, and I was nude and, naturally, not by myself. In fact, some of the photos showed me not with just one other person, but with four or five. My makeup had worn off, my eyes looked blank, and I weighed a little more, but it was unmistakably me.

I was stunned. How could this have happened? And then I started to feel angry, wondering who had sent the pictures to my boyfriend. At first I thought it must have been K, but I felt certain that it wasn't his handwriting on the envelope. So was it someone else from those days?

Then, very calmly, I wondered if my boyfriend would break our engagement as soon as he came out of the bath. He had acted perfectly normal during dinner, but I couldn't imagine that any man would remain engaged to a woman he'd seen doing things like that, without so much as a word. I resigned myself to our separation.

I stood up and went to sit by the window that looked out over the river. I wanted to get hold of myself before I saw him. I tried thinking about the negative emotions that swallow us up and death encounters that we can't even recall, but the sight of the river glistening dark outside frightened me. It flowed by at a terrific speed. I couldn't think anymore, and instead just gazed out, blankly. A small, round moon shone in the black sky, a pearl over the night lights of the city.

I opened the window, and could hear the faint sound of laughter from the street below. Oddly, the sound of the river made me think less of water than of the sound of night itself. The wind swept in and surrounded me, though I couldn't tell whether it was right there with me, or at a great distance. It felt as if the outdoors had come right into the room with me.

I sat gazing down at the river, until, finally, I heard him getting out of the bath. He walked into the living room, wearing the same pajamas as always. "It's your turn," he said with a gentle smile.

He was so matter-of-fact that it scared me. Then I realized that the letter might not have arrived that day, as I had been assuming. It might have come last week, or last month, for all I knew. If I sat there and didn't let on that I'd seen the pictures, the evening might progress as usual. At least that's what I thought, until he asked, "Is something bothering you?"

So I decided to ask him point-blank.

"When did that letter come—you know, the one on the counter in the kitchen?"

I watched the color drain out of his cheeks, and his smile disappear. The only other time I'd seen such a somber expression on his face was at the funeral.

"Last Saturday, I think it was," he answered.

"Why didn't you tell me?"

"What was I supposed to say?"

"That you want to break off the engagement, or that I make you sick, or that you're shocked. I don't know," I said. "I mean, what would it do to your family's company if those pictures got out? It'd be a huge embarrassment for your brother."

"It's no big deal."

My mind went blank. I had no clue what to do or say next.

"Why did you want to marry me?" he asked.

"I felt sure of you. I knew that it would work out," I told him.

"Well, I did too, and that's no lie."

"But this really messes everything up." I didn't even know what I wanted by then.

"Let me tell you something about myself. If I had become the president of the firm, I could have accomplished so much. I have no way to prove that, of course, but something tells me that I could have done even bigger and better things than Dad did. And, in fact, I'm not sure that my brother has any aptitude for running a business. Of course, I'll back him up in whatever he wants to try."

He continued, "I let my brother take over the

company because I want to lead my life the way I want to, and at my own pace. After Father died, everyone started grabbing for his own piece of the pie, and it was a godawful mess. I couldn't deal with it. But I guess that's what usually happens when somebody dies, especially if there's money involved.

"I'd grown up with the business, so I thought that I was comfortable in that world. I also assumed that I'd be at the top someday, but after seeing all that crap, I decided that I wanted out. Everyone told me that Father had intended for me to take over for him, and I knew that to be the case. You know, the guys at the office had been buttering me up for a long time, and when my brother noticed it, he'd start pouting.

"I couldn't stand it any longer, so I told them that I just wanted a larger share of the inheritance in exchange for not being head of the business. No one at the office could believe what I was doing. They say that nobody, absolutely nobody in his right mind gives up being president of a company.

"But I'm just not into work anymore. I'm still young and I have no ambition. Do you know what that means? It means that I'm finished as a man, I'm deadwood. I know that about myself, but I'll just keep doing what I'm doing at work. I have no choice.

"I know that it seems pathetic, having a hotshot title but spending my days shuffling paper. No ambition, no goals. I've felt that way ever since Dad got sick. I know people probably think that it's just because I'm a spoiled rich boy with nothing inside, but that's how I feel.

"So all I want to do is to see you, and be close to you. That's all. People may look down on me, but I can't help it. And as for those photos, I don't know— nothing surprises me anymore. I could tell that you were a lot younger then, and I'm sure if the guy who sent them had more recent pictures, he would have used those instead. If I thought they'd been taken recently, I'd feel differently, I'm sure, but I know for a fact that you're not leading that kind of life now."

Although he hadn't gone into great detail about the infighting at the company after his father fell ill, I had a fairly good idea of what had gone on from the rumors that were circulating when I was still working.

"And anyhow, to be perfectly frank with you, I could tell that you had a lot of experience the first time we made love," he said.

"You could?" I said with a smile.

"Of course. I knew that you'd done it a lot, more than most women."

At that moment, I was truly without words. I realized that the world didn't exist by virtue of my mind. On the contrary, he and I and everyone else were swept up in a great whirlpool, swirling around constantly and not knowing where we're bound. Our sensations of pleasure and suffering, our thoughts, none of these things can stop the motion. For the first time, I was able to step away from my imagined position in the center of the universe and see myself as part of something larger. This was my revelation, and I now felt—what? Not particularly happy or sad, but just a bit precarious, as if I'd relaxed some muscle that I hadn't needed to use all along.

"If that's the way you feel, then I will come and live with you. That's all right with you?" I asked.

"Couldn't be happier," he replied. "If nothing else, I value my ability to judge other people. You are something, you really are. When I'm with you, I feel like I'm watching a movie."

"Someone else told me the same thing once."

"And those pictures—well, I was mad at the guy who sent them, but, hey, you look pretty good in them! I wish he'd sent a couple more," he said jokingly. "You'll get chilled, sitting there by the window. Why don't you take your bath now? It'll do you good."

I shut the window, and then looked down at the river again. Unlike the river I had seen moments before, full of chaos and anxiety, the water now appeared calm and powerful, like an image frozen by a camera lens. It was peaceful, like the passage of time, flowing by, gentle and unchanging. It amazed me how utterly different things can look, just with a change of heart.

I thought about my mother too, when she stood on the bridge, holding me and staring down at the water. How had she felt when she saw my father walking down among the trees, from afar? I wondered whether she was excited to see him, or upset and angry, but then she probably didn't understand the exact nature of her feelings at the time either. And the warmth and the weight of me, a tiny baby in her arms. And how had the river looked to her after she had thrown me in, after the water had swallowed me up? Calm and clear or turbulent?

What happens to us when we hide things from others, keep them to ourselves, and then later let them go?

Suddenly it occurred to me that the river may have called me there. I would never, ever jump into the river, I promised myself. I felt sure, though, that it had summoned me to its banks, to this window, with the same pull as things that attracted me when I was younger. All those hidden forces, sinister motives, kindnesses, things that my parents had lost and found.

The river possesses the force to guide fate. I think that nature, buildings, and mountain ranges have some effect on our lives. Everything is intertwined and linked together, and within that mass of forces I have survived, and will live on, not because of anything I've decided. With that realization, I suddenly felt something shining within me.

When I looked out from that window each morning at the river, I saw the water glistening, like a million sheets of crushed gold leaf, flowing by. The light within me was something gorgeous like that. I wondered if that was what people in the old days used to call hope.

AFTERWORD TO *LIZARD*

BY BANANA YOSHIMOTO

I wrote these stories over a period of about two years. In them, I was interested in exploring time, healing, karma, and fate. I'd been thinking about the very different ways people can see their time on this earth, either as a sort of paradise, or as a living hell. To my mind, however, it's not that people live lives that are inherently good or bad. I believe that we create our own heaven or hell in the very process of becoming and being our "selves." My intention in these stories was to investigate that ongoing process, with the result that many of the pieces deal with religion and spiritual topics.

I believe that we are not born with hope, but rather that it comes to us as a transforming force. The people in my stories are encountering hope for the first time. The process of discovery usually starts when they notice something about themselves or their surroundings that they were never aware of before, or experience anew a forgotten sensation. That type of awakening compels them to act and to change things. I wanted to write about the feelings of disorientation, apprehension, and uncertainty that accompany most attempts at sorting out one's own emotional baggage, as well as the feelings of liberation that some people have at crucial times in their lives.

These stories appeared in a variety of places. First, I wrote "Helix" as an afterword to *The Moon over Troy* by Hara Masumi, and I am grateful for her permission to include it in the present volume. "Newlywed" was serialized on posters aboard the Higashi Nippon Japan Railway trains from January through March 1991, with illustrations by Ms. Hara. This story actually rode the rails around Tokyo.

For "A Strange Tale from Down by the River," I borrowed the title from a song by the Tights, and was also inspired by several images in that piece. My gratitude to the composer Isshiki Susumu for his fine song.

I would like to thank everyone who encouraged me when I was working on this book. I had fun writing these stories. I would especially like to express my appreciation to my dedicated editors at Shinchosha, Imada Kyojiro and Mochizuki Reiko. Also, thanks to Tanaka Hideki for the cover art for the Japanese edition.

Thank you to all of my readers for your letters and your thoughts. With your encouragement, I hope to continue to write interesting stories.

An early spring evening, at the office
(I'm on my way to a Sonic Youth concert!)

AFTERWORD TO THE
AMERICAN EDITION

I'm so happy that three of my books have already been translated in the States. The first two, *Kitchen* and *N.P.*, were novels. *Lizard* is my first collection of short stories.

During the period when I was writing these stories, I experimented with a number of different narrative approaches. I'm not confident about the success of my attempts, but I feel a great attachment to this volume anyway, because it reminds me of both the pleasure and the concerns I had during that time in my career.

I love the idea that these translations will allow many people outside of Japan to sample my writing. It is a privilege to have a new and different audience.

I would like to express my appreciation to the

translator of *Lizard*, Ann Sherif, who built that bridge spanning the Pacific. Also, my deepest gratitude to everyone at the Japan Foreign-Rights Centre in Tokyo and Grove Press in New York.

Since the first translations of my work appeared, I've received many letters from readers around the world, which have been a great source of strength and encouragement for me. Through such correspondence, I have come to understand that many of us living at the end of the twentieth century share similar thoughts and feelings, despite the great distances separating us. Many thanks to my readers everywhere.

I would like to dedicate this book to the memory of the late Kurt Cobain. Without his music, I could never have written these stories. He is gone now, but his songs remain with us.

Until our next meeting . . .

BANANA YOSHIMOTO
September 1994